ERIK AND DAKOTA WITH THE ANGELS

written by
Colleen Edwards

illustrated by Jack Foster

D1502685

Halo
PUBLISHING
INTERNATIONAL

To contact author:
colleenedwards333@gmail.com

ISBN: 978-1-63765-103-2
LCCN: 2021916501

Halo Publishing International, LLC
8000 W Interstate 10, Suite 600
San Antonio, Texas 78230
www.halopublishing.com

Printed and bound in the United States of America

This book is Dedicated to Sandra, Kim, Ashleigh and JJ – with All of my Love.

PROLOGUE

Somebody kept calling my name. I was in that kinda space between sleeping and waking and the sound was dream-like. Far away and foggy. And then a hand clamped onto my shoulder, shaking it really hard, and I started coming to.

"Erik! Erik! Wake up!! Look! What's going on?!"

I opened my eyes to see my little brother, Dakota, staring at me with the biggest eyes I had ever seen. On anybody. Eyes filled with incredible amazement, fear and excitement – all at the same time.

"Come on, get up, Erik! Look! Look!"

"What?!" I yelled at him. "What is so important that you had to almost tear my arm outta' the socket? Geez, 'Kota," I said, rubbing my right arm and shoulder, "calm down."

But all he could manage was to point. With his left hand on my shoulder and his mouth hanging wide open, he raised his right hand and just pointed. He pointed straight ahead, then up, then to the left, and my eyes followed his finger in every direction it went. And then, my mouth was hanging open too, and my eyes must've looked about as crazy as 'Kota's.

"What the..?" was all I could get out.

"I know, Erik, I.." was the best Dakota could manage.

I turned to look at my brother. He had on jeans, a dark green tee-shirt from our football team, and the red Chuck Taylors he had begged Mom for last year. I looked down at my own body, and saw that I had on jeans, too, and the red tee-shirt from our team. As usual, my black high-top Adidas tennis shoes weren't tied, but that was the least of my problems then. Cuz now, I could see on Dakota's back, and outta' the corner of my eye sticking out around my own shoulder, wings.

That's right - bright and shiny golden wings were on both of our backs, looking a little like a million tiny Christmas balls all blinking at once, they were so bright. I looked up at 'Kota's head and there was a yellowish round light hovering about six inches above the top of his head too. I pointed up at it, still not saying a word, and 'Kota pointed above my head, shaking his own head up and down like "Yep. You got one too."

We looked at each other; I looked around me at other people flying by with their wings blinking; and it struck me that there were no houses or apartments around us. No cars were whizzing by and there wasn't a lot of noise, like there always was on our street in Northeast Washington DC. There was only a kind of soft music coming from somewhere. I looked down, then, at where I was sitting, and what I had been laying on, and realized it was a big fluffy white cloud. Now, I was totally freaked out.

Just when I thought I was gonna' lose it, for real, Mama came floating toward me. Mama. Floating! Her back was blinking too… Golden shiny wings and the brightest smile I had ever seen on her, in all of my eleven years. I knew she could see the pure terror on my face and she grabbed me in a big ole hug. With her other arm she pulled Dakota in and just hugged us, for a long time. I started to calm down and could feel that 'Kota was too. We both just kinda melted into Mama's arms and when we had relaxed a little bit, she bent down and started speaking softly, reminding us of what had happened. How we had gotten where we were now.

"But we're safe now," she told us. "And we're together, in this beautiful place. I just saw my grandparents, and I am so happy to see them! Come on, you never got to meet them."

And we all floated off – me and 'Kota looking at each other while we tried out this new way of getting around. Floating.

"What the.." again came out of my mouth. It was easy, though, and we learned fast. It was kinda like a butterfly - lying flat or upright – and gently moving our wings, back and forth. 'Kota did a kind of somersault, only turning side to side instead of front to back, and I cracked up laughing, watching him do that. We both started laughing then and couldn't seem to stop. Mama looked at us and smiled; happy, I know, that we were getting adjusted to whatever this place was.

It felt good, I could tell, to all of us. And as we looked around, Mama saw and recognized other people that she knew, smiling, beaming, and looking so happy to see us. There was our great grandmother – "White Grandma" as her older great grandchildren had called her because she was so very light-skinned - and there was great granddaddy with her. Me and Dakota hadn't known either of them, cuz they'd left the Earth before we were born, but we'd seen tons of pictures, and heard lots of stories about both of them. We immediately recognized them and were so excited. Our mom, Erika, was over-the-moon! She adored her grandmother and grandfather. What could be better than seeing them again?

What a cool thing, meeting our great-grandparents and Mama introducing us to lots of our other relatives. Uncle Tom, Aunt Olive, Aunt May. Our cousin Wanda. And lots of others. Wow. I didn't realize we had come from such a big and happy family! They were all laughing and hugging us, and it was wonderful to see them all. I looked at Dakota and his grin was just about as big as mine felt.

And then we all sensed it. I don't know if it was a sound, or just a really strong feeling, but we all seemed to get it at the same time, and we looked down.

The Earth was right below us, looking pretty much just like those globes and balls of the Earth that you see everywhere. We were kinda hovering over it, and could make out what was going on. More as we got closer. There was this sound and a really sad feeling that was coming up from the Earth like a big strong wave, and it hit us. As lovely as this moment was for us – sparkling and floating and seeing our loved ones we realized: we had left a family, a city, and even a country; sad and crying over us. There was shock and disbelief that everyone seemed to be feeling, and we could feel it, clearly, from where we were. As we all looked down at the Earth, we could see that our leaving it had been shocking and devastating to so many people. The weight of the sadness and grief was even causing changes in the weather. Bolts of lightning were shooting all around the DC area, and the birds and the deer were still. They had stopped moving and making noises and were quiet, listening, wondering what it was that had made the humans so upset. Why so many tears were flowing and so many hearts were breaking.

Seeing the tears and the suffering was hard. And we could see, now, just how much we were loved.

CHAPTER ONE

We remembered it all, then; what had happened, and knew that we were no longer living on the Earth and were all lit up and shiny because we were now with the angels. We were, in fact, angels our selves.

My throat got tight looking down on Earth and all of our family and friends and my stomach felt funny. Like butterflies were swimming around in it. Even though we were with each other and our Mom and other family, we could see how much everybody that loved us was hurting.

"'Kota, look – there's JJ." Our brother, 16 years old, 6 foot 4 and our hero, had tears running down his face as he sat in the empty bleachers behind his school, staring into space.

"He looks terrible, Erik, like he hasn't slept in forever, and so mad."

Angel-tears rolled down Dakota's face too, as we floated down to our brother and sat on either side of him. It was getting dark and we knew he had a long walk still ahead of him to get home. He should've left a long time ago.

"I always wanted to get as tall as JJ, Erik. Do you think we can still grow, now that we're angels?"

I think about it – and realize there's so much we don't know yet about being here - wherever "here" was now. "Hmmmmm…

guess we'll just hafta see, Buddy. Whatever happens, though, we're gonna' do it together. Just like always."

We looked down at Aunt Mildred and Uncle Alfred's house and there was our little sister, Bijou. Not quite three and really not knowing what was going on – just that suddenly, we weren't there anymore.

"I'm so glad, 'Kota, that Bijou's staying with Aunt Mil and her family, but I can't imagine how weird it must be for her – not having us around and not understanding what happened."

"I know, Erik. I was thinking the same thing. You think there's some way we can let her know we're still around her?"

And Grandma. Our sweet, sweet grandmother – who loves us so much and took such good care of us – buying us whatever we needed and being a soft place for us to land when things got too hard sometimes around the house.

"Erik, look at Grandma," Dakota said, and I looked down to where he was pointing. She was sitting in a chair with her eyes closed and her arms folded across her stomach, rocking back and forth and making sounds like she was in pain.

"Grandma, Grandma!" I started shouting – "we're OK! We're right here, in this beautiful place and we can still see you! Don't be sad, Grandma, we're fine. Honest. And everybody's here with us. Your mom and dad and everybody!"

But Grandma couldn't hear us and now tears started rolling down my face. I looked at my little brother and we hugged each other. Whew. This was gonna' be tough, I could see that now. All of our family and friends looked like their hearts were gonna' break they were so sad.

"Hey! Hey you all! Look at us. We're still alive, sort of. We can see you and we're all together and this place is wonderful! Don't cry!"

But nobody looked up. They just kept on crying. I wish they could hear me. I want to tell them that the hard times are over for us. I want them to laugh – and remember how silly I used to be sometimes. Like when I tried to teach the whole family that crazy dance one Thanksgiving up at Aunt Toni's house. They were so funny to watch – tripping all over their feet!

And when me and Dakota would play tricks on everybody and have them all laughing their heads off. I wish they'd think about all that, and laugh at me instead of crying. But I understand. I'd be sad, too, if I lost any of them. Even my teachers and classmates are crying, and people that we didn't even know are sad.

'Kota looked over at me while I was still looking down, twisting my hands together and biting my bottom lip. He was the one that told me that I always do that when I'm sad or thinking too hard. He came over and pulled on my sleeve and pointed up. A gazillion angels, it seemed, were coming in our direction. Tons of them – all ages and all colors. Babies, old people, teenagers and even kids our age. Wow. And dressed in all kinds of clothes. I guess some of them were clothes they had worn in the places they lived in on Earth. A lot of them had on all white. And nobody had on shoes. One man had on a green shirt and looked like he was about two hundred years old in the face, but was floating around, flapping his wings, like a little baby. They were all laughing and smiling at us. Everybody was so nice, and it felt like everybody loved us, and they didn't even know us! Mama and our great grandparents were with them, and were smiling at us too.

I looked at my brother and best friend. "What do you think about all this 'Kota? This is wild!"

"It sure is," Dakota said. "And I like it!"

'Kota was always kinda like an angel anyway. Quiet, with those big, deep eyes and sweet, soft way, I'm sure he feels right at home. I've heard people call him an angel while we were still down there on the Earth. Even the nuns at the Catholic school we went to said that, and they should know!

And smart as a whip! At the top of his class always, with nothing but A's on his report card. Mama and his teachers used to talk about him being a genius, cuz he never seemed to study, though he loved books, and he always did great on those tests that everybody in the country had to take. 'Kota loved math, too, which totally messed with my head!

"So you like it here, huh, Buddy?" Even though 'Kota and I are only a year apart, I've always felt like a real big brother to him. Like I have to protect him cuz he's so soft, and there're a lot of hard people out there. But now, we're somewhere where everything around us seems to be soft.

"Yeah Erik I do. I've never felt anything like this. Like when all those angels came around us, it felt like I was being washed or something, with love! I used to feel a little bit like that sometimes when we went to church, or when I was outside in the park or near a lake or something. But nothing like what this felt like. Like they were all shooting love at us by just looking at us."

"You felt that too, huh? It's weird! And those smiles! Like none of them have any problems and they're all just happy! Not like it was walking down the street on Earth! Boy – everybody's faces always screwed up, and looking mean. Hardly anybody smiling at you, or even looking at you. That's sure a change up here.

And did you see Mama's face? I don't think I've ever seen her so happy. Maybe when Bijou was born, but not since. It was always so hard for her; I could see that even though she tried to hide it from us."

"Yep. I noticed that too Erik; and could you hear some of them talking – without even moving their lips?! What was that about?"

"Yeah, I saw that too. And guess what? You aren't moving your lips now!"

Me and 'Kota 'bout fell out laughing when we realized that neither one of us was opening our mouths to talk. We were just looking at each other and thinking what we wanted to say and hearing each other's words in our minds. Geezy-Peezy what in da world was going on here? We were in a new place for sure!

I wonder if there's anybody here I can play football with, and video games? Are there even TV's, or iPods here? I throw my hand up in front of my face like I'm holding a microphone and start singing and doing my favorite Michael Jackson dance routine.

"Oh my goodness – there he goes," Dakota shouts, his eyes filled with joy. "Maybe here you can finally be a star, and give your own concert!"

I hit what I think is my best moon-walk ever, and twirl around kicking my leg in the air. Michael Jackson would be proud. Dakota and I have ourselves a good laugh, both of us I know, feeling like - even though we were in a different place - we were still the same old silly us.

"'Kota, I know what you're gonna miss the most," I say to him.

"What?"

"Your books, Man! How you gonna' make it without sticking your head in some book like you do all the time? We might have to make some books for you outta' these clouds, or something!"

I could tell 'Kota hadn't thought about that yet, cuz his eyes got big and he looked shocked. A life without books? It was something he would never have imagined. I saw his eyes well up with tears and he looked away.

"Hey – no worries, Dude! You know if there is one book in this place we're gonna' find it. And if not, we'll make some, or find something else that you will love just as much. I promise!"

'Kota didn't look convinced, and I was sorry I had brought it up. He would've realized it sooner or later though.

"Come on, let's go cruising and see what we can see."

CHAPTER TWO

I'm glad since I'm not on the Earth anymore that at least I'm here with 'Kota and Mom and all these really nice angels. I keep forgetting that I'm supposed to be one now, too. Am I an angel forever now? What do angels do? Do we still have to go to school? I hope not, though I know 'Kota would be happy to go. They really loved him at his school, and planted a tree for him after we left Earth. I used to go to that school too, until Mama put me in a different school last year. She thought I'd do better in a smaller school - that was more artistic and creative - like me. They liked me a lot there, too, and even though I'd only been there for six months, everybody knew me and had good things to say about me. They had this fantastic balloon party for me after I left Earth. Everybody in the school – all the teachers and the students and my grandma and aunts and cousin – had these green balloons and they all went outside the school on 16th Street – right up the street from the White House, and let them go. I wonder if Mr. Obama and his family saw them? I was watching from up here and it was so cool! The balloons spread out all over the place! I wanted to let them know I saw them but didn't know how to tell them. All my classmates went up to my grandma and started hugging her and telling her all about me and how much they liked and missed me. That made grandma cry, but I think she was happy that I had so many friends and they liked me so much. It's hard, when you're ten or eleven years old, to lose somebody. I used to get sad just hearing about people passing away, even if I didn't know them.

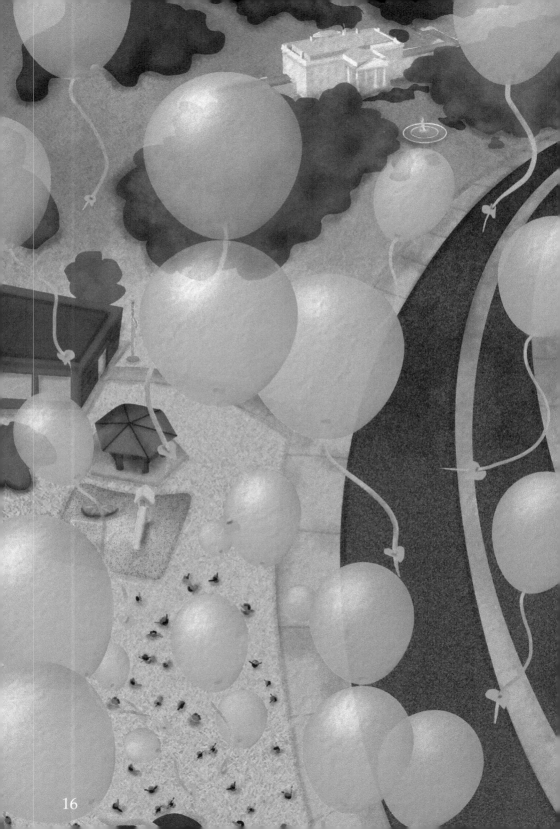

I wonder how much time has passed since we've been here? And where is "here", anyway? Since we're not walking on the Earth anymore but we're close and can still see it and everybody and everything on it, I don't really know where we are. We can float and fly, which is really cool and I haven't seen the game-boys or iPods yet, but it seems like there's a lot of new stuff that we'll have to explore. It's fun just being able to be anywhere we want to be and see everything and everybody we want, all at once! We just have to think about it and we can float there! Wow! Just like magic!

Me and 'Kota have been calling it Angel-Land since we got here, cuz that's all there is around us – people who used to live on the Earth like we did, and some who never did but always hung around Earth, looking out for and taking care of the people down there. Those angels that help people on the Earth seem something like Super-Angels, cuz their wings are much bigger and their lights look much brighter than the others. Sometimes, I even see people who still live on Earth but come up here when they go to sleep at night on Earth. They wake up in the morning and think they've been dreaming, but really they were here. I can't wait to tell them that one day.

Most of the angels I've heard talking seem to call this place "Here", and they call Earth "There."

Like, they'll ask each other, "Where were you before you started living Here?"

Or they'll say, "I'm going There for a visit", which means to visit with people on Earth for awhile.

It's kinda funny to me that they would say "living" when on Earth we would say people weren't living anymore when they were Here. But we really are living, and in the same bodies. They're just lighter, more transparent. Like, see-through.

17

"Erik look – how beautiful everything is!" Dakota was pulling on my shirt-sleeve and dragging me with him as he was twirling around in a circle – pointing all over the place. Up, down, to the right and to the left. His face was actually glowing and his eyes looked the happiest I'd ever seen them. We'd been spending so much time kinda in shock and trying to figure out where we were and what it was all about, that we hadn't really checked the place out.

"Wow, man! I don't believe this Dakota. Are we in a painting, or what?"

"Look at the trees, Erik, and the colors of the flowers. I've never seen colors like that before. There are colors that aren't even in the biggest crayon box!"

"And look at how big the butterflies are, 'Kota, and how pretty! And the rivers and those huge mountains over there. Good googa-mooga! Even in those National Geographic magazines we used to look at – there wasn't anything that looked like this!"

We just stood there for awhile, taking it all in. I got goose bumps and I could feel my heart beating really fast. I could see how excited Dakota was too. His eyes were jumping from one scene to the next, trying to take it all in.

"And the animals, Erik. All of them moving around together with no fighting. I can't believe it. There's even dolphins and whales jumping up over there. Look!"

We were dizzy now, from turning around and from all that we were seeing, and we plopped down on a cloud, just as an airplane was whizzing by, beneath us.

"Whew," Dakota kinda whistled, after he'd caught his breath, "this is amazing, Erik. Is this where we live now? Is this paradise, or what? What do you think? How could there be such a beautiful place right here near Earth and we never heard about it before?"

"Dakota, all I know is, this is the most awesome place I could ever imagine. Animals and oceans and mountains and trees and flowers - all in the same place? And can you hear that sound that's kinda everywhere all at the same time? You know the kind of music I like – and this ain't it! But they sure are the most beautiful sounds I've ever heard!"

"And the smells, Erik. It smells kinda like cookies baking, don't you think?"

"It smells like flowers to me. Or like somebody sprayed the most gorgeous perfume everywhere."

We flopped down on our backs on the cloud and just looked up, trying to take it all in, breathing hard. We hadn't seen much of Mom since we got here. Since it was so safe and she didn't have to worry about us, she was out and about, seeing all her old friends and relatives. And we were taking it all in, and trying to figure it all out, by ourselves.

Wiped out from all that we had been checking out, and enjoying the soft cloud we were laying on, we were interrupted, suddenly, by a voice.

"So what's up, Lazy Bones?" it asked. The voice was coming from a girl, and we both sat straight up and saw this angel-girl, floating over us with a big grin on her face.

"Nothing much" I answered. "What's up with you?" She was the first angel to actually speak to us. All the others would float by and smile, and shoot us that love energy that they all seemed to have, but none of them had actually stopped and said anything. 'Kota and I had pretty much been on our own – looking around and trying to figure this thing out.

"I'm Meranda. Who're you? And how long have you been Here?"

"I'm Erik, and this is my brother Dakota. I'm not sure how long we've been Here – not long, though. What about you?"

"I'm not exactly sure either, but it's been quite a while. I usually tell time by looking back at Earth and seeing the changes there. My little sister was four when I came Here and she's about ten now, I think." Meranda ran her hand through her thick hair and kinda twisted her mouth to the side when she talked about her little sister. The grin was gone from her face.

"So can you tell us about being Here?" Dakota asked, squirming around and looking anxious. "What it's like, what do we do every day, who's who and all of that?"

"Yeah, sure, little guy, I can fill you in on what I know. Let me cop a squat here on this cloud with you all and I'll share some knowledge" Meranda said.

"Little guy?" Dakota and I looked at each other and rolled our eyes. Who did this girl think she was, anyway, with her big yellow hair sittin' up just as high as her attitude? Her legs were long and she was pretty tall, but she couldn't have been more than twelve! Acting like she was grown!

"Move over" she said, and sat down between us, crossing those long legs Indian-style. "So what you wanna' know?" she asked, "and why are you all Here anyway?"

Dakota and I told her our story and she told us about her illness, and that she had grown up in French-speaking Africa, in a place very different from how we had grown up in the city.

"What do you do all day?" 'Kota wanted to know. "And do you go to school Here?"

I laughed to myself watching them cuz without realizing it, we were communicating just like all the other angels now, without opening our mouths. Just turning to look at the person we were speaking to and saying what we wanted to say in our heads. And hearing them without their opening their mouths either. What the sam-hill was going on? Is this what telepathy means? Good lord! Wait 'til I get to see Brandon and all those guys again from our neighborhood. They will not believe this one!

Meranda was talking. Well, sending messages or whatever it is we were doing. "We do whatever we want to do. I visit with other angels, float back There a lot and see my friends and family; I'm taking music lessons and I sing in the celestial choir. We have concerts once a month. You should come. There are classes you can take on lots of different things too. People who could do certain things when they were There teach classes to anybody who wants to learn those things. And there are also classes that help us look at our lives when we were There and what choices we might have made that weren't so great and how we can change the way we were if we need to, and become better."

"Better for what?" I wanted to know. "Better angels, or are we going back to Earth and be better? Aren't all these angels perfect? Why do we need to get better?"

"Oh Erik, I can see you've got a whole lot to learn while you're Here. And no – we don't necessarily stay Here forever. Really, I don't know everything about it all, but I do know that we can always be better. Whether we're Here or There. We keep learning and keep trying to be better people, or angels, or souls, or whatever you wanna' call us. But come on, I wanna show you something. We can talk more later."

CHAPTER THREE

"Look. Over there. Underneath that big tree right there. See those people sitting on the grass?"

Me and Dakota had floated along-side Meranda, not knowing where she was taking us, and I hardly paid attention to the flight cuz I was so busy laughing to myself about her hair! Oh my god, it was huge, and as the breeze was moving through it, it got bigger, and it looked like she had a big yellow clown wig on her head. I looked at 'Kota, trying to catch his eye and make him look at her hair, but I could see he was fascinated by her, and was practicing the little bit of French that he knew, with her.

"Bonjour", he said, grinning like he had won the lottery.

"And bonjour back to you", Meranda responded. "Ca va?"

"Huh?"

He was lost already.

"Look", Meranda pointed, "at the lady down there in the green dress."

I tore myself away from looking at her hair and looked down at the ground. We were only about twenty feet higher than these three people – a man and two women - who were sitting on a blanket under a great big oak tree, talking.

"Yeah and so what?" I wanted to know. "Do you know them?"

"No, I don't. But watch."

23

All of a sudden Meranda started flapping her right hand, like she was waving away a fly or something. As we watched, the lady in the green dress started looking around her, like she was feeling something. The other two kept on talking and the green dress lady looked at them and said, "do you feel that? Like the wind has picked up?" She started to stand up.

The other two looked at her and at the same time, said "no."

But the green dress lady had gotten up by then and her hair had started moving like it was in a heavy wind and then the bottom of her dress started flying around her legs. I looked at Meranda and now both of her arms and hands were flapping along with her wings and she was cracking up laughing! Dakota's eyes were as wide as saucers, staring at the lady.

Green dress lady's eyes were 'bout as big as 'Kota's and now so were the other two people's. They had stopped talking and just stared at her while she was trying to grab at her hair and her dress at the same time, to keep everything from moving. Suddenly, Meranda stopped with the flapping and at the exact same moment, green dress lady's hair and dress stopped moving too. She just stood there and the other two got up and they just stood there too. The three of them looked at each other, then looked around them, then back at each other.

As we started to float away, I looked back and the man had reached down and picked up the blanket and they all had started walking away. Fast. Nobody said a word.

Meranda was bending over laughing her head off as she floated, her clown wig of a hairdo shaking up and down.

"What in the world was that?" I yelled at her. I knew I'd just met her, but I couldn't help myself yelling. I guess I was pretty shook up by what I'd just seen. 'Kota, however, was still quiet, and was just floating along, looking stunned.

Meranda stopped floating and stood straight up in the air. "What!? You didn't get it? I was just trying to show y'all something. That we can still communicate There. We can affect things and people. You need to know that. What? You mad or something? Or scared?" The blond puffy hair was moving up and down while she glared at me. I've gotta' remember to ask her how she wound up with blond hair, coming from Africa. But now, I've gotta' get her straight.

"No girl, I'm not mad and I'm sure not scared! I guess I'm just shocked. How'd you do that? That was you, right, making her dress and stuff move?"

"Yeah, how'd you do that? Man!" Dakota was coming out of his shock and joined in. "Did you see her face?" He started laughing and I did too. It had been pretty doggone funny!

The three of us kinda fell apart then and we laughed until my stomach was hurting and I actually felt a tear coming down my face. I wiped it off and felt shocked, cuz I wasn't one who usually cried, and didn't know that I could cry, now, as an angel, even though I saw 'Kota cry when we first got Here. Hmmm, something else I'll have to ask about later. But for now – "tell us, tell us Meranda. How'd you do that?"

"It's easy. Our bodies aren't as thick as they used to be, but we still have power. We can still make things happen, and make people on Earth feel us. Sometimes even see us. It's easy. You can do it too. You'll see."

Dakota and I looked at each other like 'yeah, sure.' We were new to this angel-business and what we'd just seen looked like something out of a movie. I had liked to play around when I was still on Earth, and tried some magic tricks I'd read about on my family and friends, but this was way outta' that league!

"OK," Meranda said, "think about somebody you know that you'd like to see, and try it out on."

'Kota immediately piped up and said "Aunt Toni! Let's go see her!"

"You think? What can we do?"

"Let's go ring her doorbell. Can we ring doorbells Meranda? Will our fingers be able to press a button?"

"I think so," Meranda answered. "I've never tried a doorbell, but I don't see why not. I've moved pictures and other things around in people's houses. Let's try it. Do you know where she lives?"

"Of course we do," I said. "In Silver Spring, Maryland, not far from where we used to live." 'Kota and I had hovered around our home town a lot since we'd been in Angel-Land, so we knew the way. "Come on."

After just a short float from where we were (I was amazed that we could move ourselves so fast with this floating business), we were hovering over Aunt Toni's seven-story brick apartment building.

CHAPTER FOUR

"Hey," Dakota said "it's just about the time Aunt Toni is watching that house program she likes. The one where people are looking at different houses and deciding which one they should buy. She should be home, don't you think?"

"Well, we'll just have to see, huh?" The sun had gone down and she should be home from work, but I was starting to get a little nervous. I mean, we had gone to visit our family and friends quite a lot since we'd been Here, but we'd never tried to make them see or hear us, and I didn't know how that would be. Sometimes, when we visit people, it seems like they can almost tell that we're there. They'll kinda look around – like they're thinking about us – and sometimes even look right in the direction where we are – like they can see us. But we didn't think we could move anything or make a noise or something so they could hear us. This would be different. And even for Mr. Macho Man me, it was kinda scary. But I couldn't let my little brother and this smarty-pants girl know that.

"Come on. She's on the sixth floor."

We floated through the brick outside wall of the building and through to the sixth floor hallway. It was quiet, like it always was when we visited Aunt Toni. 'Kota asked her once if she was sure anybody else lived on her floor. It sure wasn't this quiet in the building that we had lived in. Then we heard a dog barking one time and figured there must be somebody else living there. "Unless," I said to 'Kota, "the dog is paying the rent."

All three of us were quiet as we floated down the hall to Aunt Toni's door. Even Meranda. I think she was a little nervous too, though I'm not sure why she would've been. She was running her hand through her hair again, and Dakota was just looking straight ahead, like a horse with one of those blinder things on. We stopped outside her door, number 617, at the end of the hallway.

"Go ahead," Meranda said. "Press the button."

"I don't think we should do it," Dakota said, looking down at the rug on the hallway floor, and frowning. "We might scare her, or she might not even be home."

I yanked on the back of his green tee-shirt, right below the neck. I was getting my nerve back. And we had come this far. We couldn't turn back now!

"Come on! It'll be fun! And you know she believes in all kinda weird stuff. She might get it."

'Kota looked at me with those puppy-dog eyes, knowing he wanted to do it and forgetting for a minute how much he loved every adventure I dragged him in to. When they were over, that is, and we hadn't gotten either in trouble or hurt. His eyes starting lighting up and he finally said "Alright! Shoot! Come on. Let's do it!"

There was only one apartment across from Aunt Toni's place and it seemed all quiet there. As we leaned in to her door, we could hear the TV, and just like 'Kota said, it seemed like people were inside a house, talking about the master bedroom and the color of the paint on the walls. Meranda started grinning. "You're right! She's there, and watching her favorite show! Go on. Hit it."

I put my finger on the doorbell and I could hold it there. It didn't just go through like I thought it might. I could feel it and it felt just like it would've felt when I was living on the Earth. "Wow," I said softly to myself, "this is cool." I pressed on the button.

"Brinnnnnngggggg. Brinnnngggggggggg…." It was ringing. Oh my god. This was really happening. 'Kota was jumping up and down and Meranda was twirling around in a circle like a ballerina.

The TV went quiet and we could hear movement on the other side of the door.

"She's coming to the door. Oh my god," Dakota was shouting. Now I was the one staring ahead like a horse in blinders.

"Shhhhhhhh, you're making me nervous. Here she comes."

"She can't hear us – so what?"

"Well shush anyway – I wanna' see what happens."

We heard the door knob turn and there was Aunt Toni. All five foot eight of her, wrapped in one of those tropical pieces of cloth she liked to wear when she was at home. She had her glasses on, so she must've been reading, too, while she was watching TV.

Not seeing anyone, she looked up and down the hall. She frowned a little, made that "hmmmm" sound in her throat then closed the door.

I put my finger on the bell and pushed it again. "Bringgggg, Brinnnngggg". I was too into it to even look at Dakota or Meranda to see what they were doing. "Brinngggg." Aunt Toni opened the door again, after we saw her eye looking out the peep hole, and stood there, with a really big frown this time. Me and 'Kota were waving our hands and shouting "Aunt Toni – it's us – we're right here", but she didn't see or hear us and shut the door, went back inside, and we could hear her fiddling with the plug for her doorbell, unplugging it and flipping the switch. She must have thought something was wrong with it.

"Let's go", I told Dakota and Meranda. "We don't wanna freak her out. We can try it again another time."

'Kota looked down and I knew he was trying to hide his face. He was really disappointed that Aunt Toni couldn't see us. We really loved her and always had a good time when we spent the night with her – going to the park and playing in the creek.

"Come on Buddy. We can come back tomorrow", I said. "And maybe we can think of something else that might work better." Meranda, 'Kota and I floated off, kinda quiet.

The next day, we went and rang again. Aunt Toni peeped out the hole, then yanked the door open looking kinda mad this time. She probably thought somebody was ringing her bell and running away. She went back in and slammed her door shut. Hard. I had a thought. I raised my finger to press the bell again and 'Kota hit my hand. "That's enough Erik, we're gonna' scare her."

But I had remembered the knock we always used to do at her door – "dum-da-da-dum-dumdum dum." She would know it was us coming and would tap the last two beats on her side of the door and we would all laugh when she opened it. I tried the same rhythm with the door bell. It didn't sound exactly like the knock, but enough. This time, she jerked the door open with the biggest grin on her face. It was like a light-bulb had gone off in her head. She started laughing. "Erika, is that you and the boys?" She looked right where we were floating and her eyes filled with tears but she had the biggest smile on her face.

"Aaaaahhhhhhh-HAH! I knew she'd get it! Woooooo-Hoo!" High fives all around! We couldn't wait to get back to Angel-Land and tell Mom.

CHAPTER FIVE

We went back and told Mama and our great grand-parents and we all had a good laugh about Aunt Toni. Her Mom, Great-Grandma Lucy said "you all picked the right one to visit. My daughter has always believed in spirits and dreams and all kinds of unseen things, so I am not at all surprised that she figured it out!"

We started spending a lot of time with Meranda after that; floating around on clouds; listening to the songs she liked to make up, and some of the ones she sang in the celestial choir. I liked to make up dances to go with her songs, and we were quite a sight, I'm sure – with Meranda's big yellow hair bouncing while she sang and pretended to play a guitar, and me hopping around with my latest dance steps.

'Kota would just laugh at us. We kept trying to get him to sing and dance with us, but the most he would do was pretend to play the drums sometimes. I knew he missed books, cuz that's all he used to do back on Earth was read, and there weren't any here. We had looked and looked. I told him he needed to make up his own stories now, so maybe he'll start doing that one day soon.

Meranda told us that the place she grew up in was called the Congo. She told us that the Congo's real name is the Democratic Republic of the Congo and it's in central Africa.

"That's a whole lotta' name," Dakota told Meranda, "I can see why you just say 'the Congo'. All the rest of that is too much!"

"Hmmmph!" Meranda grunted. "It used to be called the African Congo Free State; the Belgian Congo; Congo-Leopoldville; Congo-Kinshasa; and Zaire at different times before it was the Congo! It was Zaire when I was born."

"Wow" I said quietly, and wondered to myself why in the world a country would change its name all the time. I was kicked back on a cloud looking around at some of the birds flying around right above me, just half-listening to 'Kota and Meranda talking.

"Plus," Meranda went on, "your country's whole name is the United States of America, isn't it? That's a whole lotta name too. And you usually just say America, right, or the USA. Same thing as us."

'Kota thought about that and realized she was right and asked Meranda to teach him some more French. She could speak four or five languages – French, English, the language of her tribe, and a couple of others. She asked us how many languages we could speak and 'Kota and I just looked at each other. We didn't really know there were a whole lot of other languages. All we'd ever heard was English. Around us and on the TV. English. That was it. Meranda just shook her head when we told her that. Since then, she's been giving us French lessons and I can say "comment allez-vous" pretty good – which means "how are you?" and Mr. Smarty-Pants Dakota is saying all kinds of things with her. I shoulda' known that, as smart as he is! I'm sure if we meet somebody from Germany next week, he'll be speaking German in just a few days too!

Meranda told us that back home, her mother and her grandmother before her, had been the healers of their community. When people got sick, since they were in a small village and there were no real doctors around, her mother and grandmother would pick natural herbs and get things off'a trees, and heal people. They could even, she said, put their hands on people and just that touch, would sometimes make people well.

"Come on," I said. "Just touching somebody? You've gotta' be kidding."

"No, really," M said. "I've seen it a gazillion times. People would come to our cottage and ask for Ma-Ma, and she would take them outside to the healing hut that was right next to ours, and in just a little bit of time, the sick person would walk right out, fine! All smiling and laughing like no problem. Honest."

"Yeah, right," 'Kota mumbled. He usually got real involved in whatever Meranda was saying, but this time he barely looked up from fooling with his fingers, and kinda shook his head. He glanced over at me with a look that said "she must think we are idiots!"

I grabbed my stomach and started flying away. If I had stayed close to them, Meranda would've seen me laughing so hard if I was on Earth I know I would've peed my pants. Dakota never talked bad about anybody, and to see that look on his face 'bout slayed me.

"Well if they were healers, how come your mother couldn't heal you? Why did you have to die?" Dakota wanted to know.

Meranda's face looked like a dark cloud had passed right in front of it, and she looked down. "This disease, AIDS, was one that had never been in our country until a few years before, and Ma-Ma didn't know how to deal with it. There were medicines for it, but they cost a lot and we didn't have a lot of money. A lot of people in our village died. After she couldn't save me, Ma-Ma stopped doing healing work. Every time I go see my family There, I keep hoping she would have gone back to it. She was so good, and helped so many people."

I was sorry that I had laughed at Meranda and floated back to where they were and said "I'm sorry, Meranda. I know it must be hard on your mom."

The three of us've been talking about doing some traveling. Since we've learned that we can pretty much float around wherever we want to go, and since we were all so young when we left Earth and hadn't seen much outside of our home towns – really never saw that much inside our home towns – we've decided to do some sight-seeing. Aunt Toni used to travel all the time to all these crazy-sounding places like Vanuatu and Belize and used to tell us about them when we'd spend the night and go for our walks in Sligo Creek Park. She always said she wanted to show us some of her favorite places and since we didn't then, what better time than now?

I laid back on the soft cloud and watched these gorgeous birds – snowy owls, cardinals and red-tailed hawks – cruising around above me. Watching all those birds flying around was making me want to spread my new-found wings too.

"Hey. What say we get started on some of that traveling soon. What do you all think? Nothing much going on here right now, is there?"

We had scoped out pretty much what the scene was here. So beautiful, and so wonderful to see Mama so happy with her grandparents and some of her old friends and new ones that she had made. She was dancing again and doing some acting in some of the plays. And it was just awesome to feel all of the love that everybody here gave us. All the time! All of the angels were pleasant and loving like I had never seen anything close to while we were on the Earth and every moment of every day was so cool. Nothing to be afraid of, no hatred coming from anybody, nobody yelling and no violence. The absolute bomb! But I was feeling like I wanted to see something else. There was a whole big world out there and I was ready to experience it.

Dakota and Meranda turned around and at the same time said "Yeah, I'm ready!"

We all started laughing and high-fived each other. This was gonna' be fun! We floated off to tell Mama and the great-grands and Meranda told a few of the folks she'd gotten close with since she'd been Here and we were off. Hello and goodbye! Au revoir and sayonara! Meranda had taught us 'au revoir' means goodbye in French and I heard sayonara on a movie one time. I think it means goodbye in Japanese. Whatever it means – we're outta here!

CHAPTER SIX

We all decided that our first adventure would be to Washington DC, since that's where me and Dakota were born and lived, and see what we can see there. DC is such a pretty city everybody says, and it has so many trees and flowers, thanks, we hear, to ex-President Johnson's wife, Lady Bird (that's a funny name for a president's wife), who saw to it that lots and lots of flowers and trees were planted all around the city – and especially in the downtown area. In the springtime the famous, beautiful, cherry trees that DC got as a gift from the Japanese in 1912 start blooming all around Hains Point and the Tidal Basin, which surround the Potomac River, and what a sight to see! We went down there one year with our family and there were lots of other cars there trying to see them too. SO beautiful, with their pink and white blossoms! After the cherry trees bloom in early spring, the tulips in their reds and yellows hit the street, followed by the dogwood trees and the azalea bushes in white, pink, red and purple. The colors make my eyeballs pop and 'Kota used to ask when he was small: "Who paints all these flowers?"

Mama used to tell us about our great-great aunt Olive, who used to say a poem every Spring, that I thought was so funny: "Spring has sprung, the grass is riz, I wonder where them flowers is." We must have a whole lotta' silly people in our family. Guess that's where I get it from.

Of course, 'Kota and I just mostly knew our neighborhood when we were on Earth - Maryland Avenue North East near 19th Street – not far from Benning Road. So this would be a good chance to see all the city that we want, and show it to Meranda too.

We started out downtown near East and West Potomac Parks, where different shades of the cherry trees were showing off their blossoms, and floated close in.

"Wow," said Meranda, "we don't have trees like that in the Congo! Ils sont très jolies!"

"Huh?" I said, looking at her and rolling my eyes.

"They are very pretty" Dakota piped up, translating her French and grinning at me. I'm gonna' hurt that boy one day. I could see how happy he was already, being back close to our old home.

"Look at all those people on the little paddle boats, just cruising around looking at the trees," I told them both. "How cool is that? I heard about those boats before."

'Kota wanted to go closer to the boats, to see how they were moving so we moved in and hovered over one with four seats. It looked like a mother, father and their two daughters were inside. Up this close, we could see that everybody's legs were moving like they were on a bicycle, and that was making the little boat move forward. There was this stick-like thing that the father was pushing forward and to the sides to change direction.

We could hear what the family was saying to each other, and even some of the things that they were thinking! Wow. One of the little girls was looking kinda scary-like over the side of the little boat at the water and was thinking "I hope we aren't gonna' sink. Or turn over." She looked up at her father, worried like and he looked back at her and smiled. Inside she was thinking, "I'm sure Daddy will take care of us and not let us turn over." 'Kota, Meranda and I looked at each other and smiled. I don't think any of us realized we would be able to hear people's thoughts if we got real close to them. Wow again. This was gonna' be an interesting trip!

I told Meranda about The Awakening, a 100 foot aluminum statue that used to be down there at Hains Point, which is at East Potomac Park. It was so cool - as you rode down the street with the Potomac River on both sides and grass and a golf course in the center, when you got to the very center of the road where the river is kind of in a point, this giant silver statue of a man laying on his back with his arm up, looking like he was coming up out of the ground, was right there. It was amazing. My aunt used to take us down there all the time and said it was her favorite part of DC. When they decided to move it a few years ago she looked like she wanted to cry. "Why couldn't they put another statue at the National Harbor?" she wanted to know. "The Awakening belongs at Hains Point!" When we used to go down there, we would climb all over the statue, sitting on his hand and in his mouth. I pointed out the place where it used to be and we floated toward the Lincoln Memorial.

"Look at all these people" Meranda said – turning her head and looking behind her and to the sides, "they all come here just to look at these cherry trees?" she asked me and Dakota.

"Yep" 'Kota answered her. "Every year. It's a big thing in DC and people come from all over the world to see them. Look at how different everybody is dressed. You can tell they're from lots of different countries and places. Don't you think these trees are worth it?"

"Plus" I piped in, "it's not just the trees. All these monuments are down here too. The Lincoln, Roosevelt and Jefferson

Memorials – they were all presidents – and the Vietnam War Memorial – all those things are down here too – so people get to see them all – and the trees. And look at this beautiful Potomac River. Everything is nice here, so folks come and sightsee and take it all in." I was proud to be showing off our old city. Not that we had thought much about it when we were living there, but it was cool now, to be, kinda, the expert on it. I didn't realize I knew so much about my old city.

"Yeah, I can see why people would come" Meranda said – still looking amazed at just how many people and cars were all moving around on the ground. "It's just different for me. I come from a small village and I haven't seen this many people in my whole life, let alone in one place." She looked overwhelmed, and even a little sad.

"Come on. Look. That's the Lincoln Memorial, Meranda. Let's get closer."

The Lincoln Memorial, a humongous statue of President Abraham Lincoln sitting in a chair, is pretty awesome. There's a gazillion steps leading up to the statue and from the steps you get a really cool view all the way down past the Reflecting Pool, the National Mall - lined with all the Smithsonian museums - and to the Capitol.

I waved to them both. "Let's go down to the steps," and we floated down closer. Meranda was still looking uncomfortable, and she stayed around the edge of the steps, away from all the people that were walking up and down and sitting on them.

"Come on over here" 'Kota yelled to Meranda, who was now floating behind one of the huge columns that lined the front of the memorial. "What's the matter?"

But Meranda kept backing up, away from us and the memorial, so Dakota and I floated over to her, darting in between and around all the tourists and visitors that were up and down the steps.

"What's wrong? Why don't you come on over and see the view from the steps? It's awesome," Dakota told her. "You can see all the way down the Mall and to the Capitol."

"I can see fine from here. Too many people over there. I'm good right here, merci."

"But the people aren't in your way, you're an angel. You can go right around them if you want, or over their heads," 'Kota told her. This was the first time we had seen Meranda not acting like her loud and fearless self, big hair and all. She looked like she wanted to cry, and I could tell she was afraid of something.

I moved closer to her and put my hand on her shoulder. It was the first time I had actually touched her, and she turned her head slowly and looked at my hand. "What's the matter, Meranda? Is there something here you don't like?" I wasn't really the soft and mushy type, but this angel-girl was our friend, and I could see that something had her spooked.

She was still looking down at my hand on her shoulder and said something real soft. Both me and 'Kota got closer, cuz it was hard to hear her, with all the noise from the tourists.

"Huh?", 'Kota asked. "What did you say?"

"I said," Meranda kinda yelled, seeming more like her old self now, "that it is too many people over there! Now leave me alone and let's get to getting. I've had enough of your President Lincoln."

Dakota and I looked at each other with big eyes and raised eyebrows.

"Come on" I said, and started floating away over the Reflecting Pool and the Mall. Nobody said anything until I pointed down to the Washington Monument, the Jefferson Memorial (dedicated to President Thomas Jefferson), the White House and all the others: The Vietnam Memorial and the Roosevelt and World War II memorials. I just said each of the names of the places as we passed over them, so Meranda could know what each of them was. I could tell that 'Kota was feeling the same way that I was - proud to be showing off this part of our beautiful city. We had both been down here a few times before, with our school classes and our families, but seeing it all like this, and how much everybody down there was enjoying seeing these wonderful monuments, buildings, trees, flowers, and the river, I kinda wished we had visited it a lot more when we were on Earth.

"Does it all look like this?" Meranda finally said something. She had been just floating between me and 'Kota, looking down at everything I pointed out, but not saying anything. "Everywhere in this city – it's filled with tourists and happy people on vacation? This is how you all lived?"

Me and 'Kota looked at each other and both our faces lost the big happy smiles we had on them just a second before, when we were so proud to be showing off our city. I could see the pain in his eyes and was sure he could see it in mine.

"No, Meranda, we didn't live like this. Not even close," I told her.

This was the historic, touristy part of DC, and not where most people live, I explained. And not at all like where we had lived, me and 'Kota told her. Where we lived wasn't that far from the Capitol. You could see the Capitol Building from some of the hills around our neighborhood, but it sure doesn't look like these parts. In our old neighborhood, it's mostly old houses and lots of apartment buildings. Streets with a lot of pot-holes and a lot of liquor stores. That's one thing Mama used to talk about all the time: how come there were so many liquor stores in our neighborhood, and fast-food places, but when we drove around to some of the other neighborhoods, where the houses had nice lawns and people weren't all piled up on top of each other, there weren't many liquor stores there. Mama used to say that it was planned like that – to keep people like us – who didn't have a lot of money, drunk and unhealthy. She liked to eat a lot of healthy food and didn't want us eating junk and fast-food, but it was hard to find any restaurants or stores in our neighborhood that didn't sell greasy, fried food. No health food stores anywhere around us, and that made Mama angry and sad. It was a con.. con.. – "'Kota, what was that word that Ma used to use when she was talking about all the stuff we didn't have in our neighborhood? A con.. con.."

"Conspiracy" 'Kota piped up. "She said it was a conspiracy to keep people who didn't have a lot of money sick. Feed them bad food and alcohol and not have any good hospitals around. She really believed that."

We were sitting on the grass on the Mall, near the Capitol Building. There weren't so many people down here, and Meranda seemed more comfortable than she had at the Lincoln Memorial.

"What about in your country, Meranda", I asked her. "Do most of the people live in beautiful places like in this area?"

"Nooooooo" she said, looking down at the grass and pulling on some of the blades. "I've never seen anything like all this. In my country, most of the people live in villages that don't even have running water and lights. We have to walk to the river every day to get water. There're no buildings that look like these huge places! Everybody in my village and probably the next one could live in one of these buildings, with a whole lotta space left over. This is unreal."

"Wow", I thought to myself, "no water in the house and no lights? How could they see inside? And outside either for that matter?" I just looked at Meranda and 'Kota did too. She kept talking. Kinda soft, so we had to lean in to hear what she was saying.

"My country has had a lot of wars", she said. "There's been a lot of fighting and all kinds of other stuff that I don't even want to think about now, going on. I've seen some horrible things, and that's why I got nervous back there at the memorial. Whenever strange people came into my village, terrible things would happen to the people around me. I lost a lot of my family members because of war, and the disease and hunger that follow the fighting cuz the soldiers would eat up all our food."

Dakota put his arm around Meranda's shoulder and said "I'm sorry Meranda, that you had to go thru all that. I'm really sorry."

"I'm sorry too, Meranda, and I hope that the fighting in your country stops soon." I put my arm around her other shoulder and the three of us sat like that for a long time, not saying anything. It was starting to get dark.

CHAPTER SEVEN

All three of us were pretty worn out from all the sight-seeing we did on our first day of travel, so we decided to shoot up to a cloud and kick back for the rest of the evening.

Next day, we set out to show Meranda our old neighborhood.

"Now you'll see, M, how some people really live in this city." I was trying out calling her 'M' cuz Meranda was just too much of a mouthful. So far, she hadn't said anything about it, so I was gonna' keep it up. I did that with everybody I got close to – gave them a nickname, or shortened their names. Most of the time, it just came out when I was speaking to them – their new name. And most times, it stuck.

On the way to our old house, Dakota wanted to go by his school - Holy Redeemer- on New Jersey Avenue. He wanted to see up close the tree his schoolmates had planted for him after he left Earth. We got there and there it was! It was really cool and still had the ropes around it and sticks in the ground to help keep it up until it got bigger and stronger. There was a wooden sign that said "Dakota's Tree" and the dates he was born and the day we left Earth. 'Kota always had the best smile, and when we saw his tree, his face lit up just like fireworks he was so happy. Me and M thought it was pretty great too, and we started yelling and singing the Dakota Tree Song – made up on the spot: "'Kota's got a tree-ee; 'Kota's got a tree-ee.. Na Na Nee Na Na, 'Kota's got a tree-ee". 'Kota's eyes got really big and wet, and he got the biggest grin on his face. He even did his pretend-drum playing while we were singing his tree song. He might not always talk a lot, but his eyes always give away how he's feeling, and he sure was happy then!

New Jersey Avenue, where 'Kota's school is, is only about a mile to the Capitol Building, and we flew over the dome-shaped top of it on our way to our old home. My stomach started knotting up as we got closer to our neighborhood and I started to think about what had happened on our last day on Earth. I looked out the corner of my eye at Dakota, who was floating on the other side of Meranda, and could see the tears that were coming down his cheek. He turned and caught me looking at him and we both looked away quickly. We knew what the other was thinking, and it was hard to share those thoughts; even with your best friend and brother. The person that had gone through it with you. We didn't talk much about that day and now, seeing our old neighborhood again, it all came back. And it hurt. I didn't realize that angels could still have tough feelings.

"Look", Meranda said, and pointed down to the ground. "Those boys over there playing ball. Do you know them?"

'Kota and I looked down and there was Jayson, Billy and Darrell, tossing around a football in the street in front of our old apartment building, like we had done at least 50 million times before.

That made both of us smile, and I realized that I missed our old friends, even Darrell, who I used to get mad with all the time – cuz he was always trying to show off when we played ball, and thought he could play better than me.

It was good to see him now, though, and I thought that they all looked a little sad, and didn't seem to have the same shine on them like they used to. I guess what happened that day really did affect everybody and not just us. It must have been hard on our friends to have us snatched away. Boy. That's rough. To be ten or eleven years old and have your friends taken away so suddenly. I wanted to hug everybody and tell them we're o.k. That we're good and happy and that we'll see them again one day.

"Hey, Billy!" I started yelling.

'Kota joined in. "Jayson, Darrell, yo! Hey! Right here!"

But they kept on playing, though Darrell did kinda stop for a minute and look around, like he thought he'd heard something. When he did that, 'Kota started jumping up and down. "We're right here Darrell. Hey!" But he turned back to the others and threw the ball and 'Kota and I looked at each other, disappointed.

Meranda had been watching us and before I knew it, she started with the arm and wing-flapping business again and the football went flying in the direction Jayson had kicked it in, made a quick turn, and went back in the other direction. All by itself! Meranda was floating above the ball and making it twist and turn like a tornado had come up. Haha ha ha ha! 'Kota and I started holding our stomachs we were laughing so hard. I couldn't believe it. That'll fix Darrell. They all stopped and looked at the ball, still twitching on the ground; looked at each other and tried to figure out what the heck had happened. Nobody said a word and all of their eyes were as big as moons. Aaaaahaa ha haaaaaa!!! Now how they gonna' tell anybody else about that! We'll sit around and have a good laugh together one day, when we see each other again. I love my friends!

Me, M and 'Kota slapped high-fives all around and couldn't stop laughing.

Being back in DC and seeing all the traffic and everybody buzzing around like bees, I started remembering what it was like when we lived here. It was so different in Angel-Land. Everybody There took their time and stopped to talk and smile and moved more slowly and it just felt good. From There, when we look at Earth, and especially a busy place like DC, people look like a zillion little ants, zooming around and around and speeding like they're on a race track. I see what Mama used to mean now when she would make me and 'Kota turn off the TV or stop playing video games sometime and just have us sit down and relax; or read a book; or draw. "Something natural" she would say, and 'Kota was happy with that cuz he loved reading books anyway and I think he would rather do that than play video games anyway. He did those things mostly cuz his big brother – Me! – wanted him to. But it did feel nice to take a hot bath and put on clean pajamas and socks and just sit down and read or draw sometimes, with no TV on. I would fuss of course, but I have to admit that it was nice. And I always seemed to sleep so good on those nights, too. And have such good dreams.

CHAPTER EIGHT

Leaving our old neighborhood, we decided to show Meranda the RFK stadium, that was named for Robert Kennedy, the brother of the ex-president John Kennedy. The Redskins football team used to play there, and it wasn't far from where we used to live. M wasn't very impressed, and didn't seem to care much about football.

"Oh mon dieu," she sighed. "You all and the footballs already!" The look of boredom on her face bout slayed me. I didn't know what 'mon dieu' meant, but it didn't seem good.

"What, M? You don't like football?" I mean, it was clear that she didn't but I had to make sure. It was too hard to believe that anybody didn't like football! Dear sweet Maloney! What is up with that girl?

'Kota looked at her and kinda smiled. He loved football too, but not as much as me, I think. Both of us knew every team, every player, all the stats and even stuff that happened before we were born! Our big brother JJ taught us all that stuff, and we loved it! Well at least I thought we all did, but now, with that smile he gave Meranda, it seemed that maybe 'Kota was happy to have somebody else around that wasn't as crazed over that stuff as I was.

"Plus," Meranda went on, ignoring my question, "you all keep calling that thing that your friends were throwing around a 'football', and that is not what we call a football back home."

Her head bobbed up and down when she said 'not' – the big yellow curls on her head bouncing all over the place. I've gotta remember to ask her about that hair. "That is not a football! A football is white, it's round, and it has black marks on it. That thing back there with the pointy ends I have never seen before and it is not, I repeat, a football!"

Dakota was rolling around by now, laughing his head off and wondering, I know, how I was gonna handle this one. He wasn't able to talk and little angel-tears were running down his face.

I cleared my throat. "Ah, Meranda, excuse me, but that pointy brown thing back there with the white stripes on it was a football, ma'am. I should know." We were floating past the stadium now. "And this stadium right here is where they used to play with that pointy brown thing. That white round ball that you're talking about? That's a soccer ball, Miss Meranda, and not a football thank you very much. I know that too cuz I used to play a little soccer. Now please apologize and we can be on our way." I did a little turn in the air and threw both of my hands out, like TA-DA!

'Kota was still cracking up laughing and I swear I could see smoke coming outta Meranda's ears. When we settled down and me and 'Kota could stop laughing and Meranda wasn't so mad anymore, we talked about it, and found out that in the Congo, what we call soccer was called football, and that the Congolese were very good at soccer/football, and M actually used to play a little when she was there too. So we all had a good laugh and threatened that we would crush the other if we ever found out that we could kick a soccer ball again.

After showing M the really pretty part of DC and seeing Darrell and them, I was kinda ready to leave the city. We had stopped and were sitting on the roof of the DC General Hospital, looking around at all the busyness on that campus, and I turned to them both. "What d'ya think? You all ready to check out someplace else? Where should we go next?"

Immediately, Dakota started jumping up and down. "Jamaica, Jamaica! Do you think we could find our way there? Aunt Toni used to always talk about Jamaica, and Mama, too, cuz she visited her when she lived there. Oh let's go to Jamaica, Erik. OK?"

Meranda's eyes got big and the hugest grin started crossing her face. I guess even in the Congo she had heard about Jamaica. Shoot, everybody knew about Jamaica – no matter where you were from. Everybody had heard about Bob Marley, and they played soccer there too.

I don't think any of us had really thought this traveling thing through. We just said we were gonna' travel, but hadn't talked about to where. And now, the thought of going somewhere like Jamaica had us all pumped up. I didn't want M and Dakota to see how excited I really was. Like inside me wanting to do cartwheels up and down the hospital parking lot. Nope. I had to maintain my cool. At all times. I didn't want to start talking right away either, cuz I was sure that my voice would give away my excitement. So I just said "hmmmmmmm...", like I was thinking it over. I kinda frowned and looked down, too, so they wouldn't see my eyes. Oh my goodness! Really?! Jamaica? Aw man I was stoked.

"Well, I guess it'd be alright to check out Jamaica," I finally said, after I'd gotten myself together a little bit. "It seems like you both really want to go there. I guess that could be our first stop after this." I was hoping they couldn't see the little beads of sweat that were starting to run down the sides of my face. Shoot. I always started sweating when I got excited. It didn't matter how hot or how cold it was, I was sweating. And here I was, an angel, and still sweating. Oh my goodness. But 'Kota had looked up just as I was trying to wipe it off and he caught it. Of course he knew what that meant, but he just twisted his lips to the side, trying, I know, to hide the smile that was popping up.

"Come on," I said, standing up and stretching my arms, wings and legs, "let's go tell Mom that we're heading out."

I also knew that we needed to look at a map before we headed out, cuz, really, I didn't have a clue where Jamaica was. And I knew that 'Kota and M didn't know either. But here came Dakota "I can be the guide when we head down there. You know Jamaica is in the Caribbean Sea, right below Cuba, which is right below Florida."

Yeah, I forgot – all those books my brother read. Of course he knew where Jamaica was. He probably knew where the Queen of England's best friend's next-door neighbor's cousin lived! Geez.

"Yeah, OK, 'Kota – you lead us. Let's go tell Mom."

CHAPTER NINE

Mama was doing fine! She was spending a lot of time with her grandparents and our cousin Wanda and had connected with a friend of hers who had left Earth some months before we did. I remember when that happened. Mama was hard-of-hearing and wore a hearing aid. She spoke and could hear with her hearing aid, read lips and knew sign language too. She taught 'Kota and me some sign language, though I always wished I knew more of it. Me and 'Kota and our big brother JJ helped Mom out a lot – sometimes when she couldn't understand what people were saying to her, especially on the telephone. Not being able to hear that good didn't stop Mama though, from being a fantastic singer and dancer. Everybody said I got my talent and love of performing from her! She would do this stuff like a ballet while she was doing sign language with her arms and hands to the music. It was really beautiful and every time the family got together like for holidays or birthdays, she would sing, sign and dance for us. She also acted in plays, from the time she was in elementary school. A born actress, everybody said, and we were all so happy that after not doing it for so many years, cuz she was raising us, she had started performing with a group again just months before we left the Earth. They traveled to a few other cities and she was so happy to be back doing what she loved!

This friend of hers that she saw who is an angel now too, used to perform with her group, and was really well known in the DC deaf community – like Mom was. Oh my goodness they were so happy to see each other, and right away – they started using sign language with each other. It didn't matter that when you become an angel you really don't even have to use words anymore, unless you want to – they were just so excited to see each other that they started talking like they used to, on Earth.

I remember one time we were with Aunt Toni and she was asking us if we knew how to walk home from school, if something ever happened and the bus or Mom couldn't reach us. She wrote a letter to everybody in the family, telling us that we should all make sure we had extra food, water and supplies in the house in case there was some kind of emergency and we couldn't get stuff from the store. She said that each family should work out a plan – in case phones weren't working, on where we should meet and how we would get home from school or work. Me and 'Kota told her we knew how to get home from school, cuz we watch the way the bus or Mom goes, when they're driving. She also said that we should practice this telepathy with each other, so we could use it if we ever couldn't reach each other. I thought it sounded crazy then, but now we see that's what the angels do. Maybe it's not so crazy after all. Aunt Toni said that even when we're on the Earth, humans have a lot of powers that we don't use – like some of the super-heroes, I guess.

"So you guys are gonna' see a little of the world, huh?" Mama asked us. She had an arm around both me and Dakota and was smiling so bright it looked like stars were twinkling in her eyes. She looked so beautiful. And so happy. I love her so much.

"Yeah, Mama" 'Kota told her. "Jamaica! Can you believe that? Maybe we can see the woman you used to tell us about, who cooked you that bomb chicken and rice! Can you believe we can actually go there?!"

Mama rubbed Dakota's head and kissed him on the cheek. "Yes, baby, that is wonderful. You will love Jamaica. You two look out for each other and have some fun. I'm fine."

We kissed and hugged our great-grandparents and Miss M floated up after saying 'so long' to some of her friends and fellow choir members. "Let's get this party started", she said, blond clown-wig-looking hair bouncing up and down all over the place. "Onward and forward. Allons-y!"

I looked at Dakota with a frown and he whispered "it means 'let's go'." This girl better stop with the French already. The angels seeing us off started waving and throwing kisses and saying "have fun. Be safe. Tell everybody hi", as we were floating off. Woooo-Hoo!

CHAPTER TEN

All of us were pumped. This was it! Hittin' da road – or da sky, as it were. Big grins were on all of our faces and we started floating in a kind of formation. Nobody arranged it – we just did it. Me and 'Kota on the ends and Meranda in the middle – a little ahead of us. Sorta' like an upside-down 'V'. 'Kota's green shirt, my red one, and the printed dress that M had on made a nice contrast. Or at least I thought it did, as I checked us out, feeling rather grown as we headed on our big adventure!

And so we cruised, checking out the scenery and feeling so excited! We hadn't gotten very far, just far enough that we couldn't see the angels we were leaving behind, and Meranda suddenly stopped. "Listen. You all hear that?"

I hadn't heard anything and was just about to pull on her arm when all around us, all of a sudden, and out of nowhere, were streams of people – old, young and in-between – coming up from the Earth and heading in the direction of Angel-Land. We just stopped and looked, mouths hanging open, as babies and little girls, boys, teenagers, men and women, shot past us – looking stunned and in shock. We must've looked that same way too.

"What the..?" I couldn't say any more than that. It must've been hundreds, or thousands, of people flying past us, heading in the direction we had just left.

"Oh my god," Dakota was mumbling.. "what is.."

"Shhhhhhhh!" Meranda had kinda come to, and was shushing me and Dakota. "Quiet. I wanna hear this."

I didn't know what she could hear, I couldn't hear anything but the 'whoooosh' as folks flew by me, but I kept quiet. 'Kota did too, and we just stared at what was happening around us. They seemed to fly by for a long time – I don't know how long it was – but finally it stopped. The last of them flew by and we all looked down to see if any more were coming. It didn't look like there was. And I couldn't hold it in any longer.

"What was that and who were they?!" I yelled. I was flabbergasted, shaken up, and felt like I was in a dream or something.

"I listened," Meranda said, "and they were all thinking the same thing. It seems like they were all living in Haiti, and there must've been an earthquake, and they all were caught in it and died at the same time. Oh my goodness. Wow."

"You could actually hear what they were thinking?" 'Kota asked her. "All I could hear was like the wind, whooshing, as they went by. How can you hear them?"

"Just like we do in Angel-Land, and some people can do on Earth – telepathy. Don't worry, when you've been an angel for a longer time, it'll come easier to you too. And when people are in shock like they all were, their emotions sound louder. It was like they were screaming their thoughts, even though they weren't opening their mouths."

"Oh my goodness," I said. "That must be awful. Poor Haiti."

"Yes," Meranda went on, "and they're all scared right now. Cuz it happened so suddenly. Once they get to Angel-Land, though, and all the other angels welcome them, and they realize what happened, and start to see their friends and relatives, they'll start to settle down. Wow, I'm so sorry for them, and for the people they left behind."

"Yes," 'Kota said, "the whole country must be in shock."

Earthquakes are terrible, cuz you don't know, mostly, when they're gonna' happen – and you're just going about your business, or sleeping, when Bam! The ground starts shaking.

We talked about going back to Angel-Land to help welcome all the new angels, but decided to keep going, and to stop by Haiti on our way to Jamaica. The islands were really close to each other, 'Kota told us. So we kept on floating, quiet, with everybody thinking about what we'd just seen, and remembering, I'm sure, our first times entering Angel-Land.

We took our time, heading down the East Coast of the United States toward the Caribbean Sea, where Haiti and Jamaica are. On our way there, all of the places that we flew over looked and felt so different from each other. Like, we could tell if we were over a big city, or farmland, or mountains or whatever, cuz of how it looked and felt. In the cities, there was a lot of dark, smoke-like air – I guess from pollution and all and it was kinda hard to see down to the land and the people. And it felt and sounded funny too. Like a lot of static and jumbled noise and you could actually feel a lot of emotions, like anger and sadness and even sometimes happiness, jumping up into the air. Like all those feelings were streaming up off of the sidewalks. And I guess it didn't help that everybody had a cell phone, I-pod, game boys and all that stuff, cuz the energy from all of that seemed to fill up the air too. When we floated over farmland and big rivers and mountains, it felt different. Peaceful, and the air felt calm. The mountains were different even from the rivers and oceans and farmland. Each of the places had their own feel. It was so interesting. I never would've thought about any of that.

We floated over the southern part of the United States, and slowed down as we got to Florida and saw all the people on the beaches.

"Wow", 'Kota said, "look at how long those beaches are! I've never seen anything like that before. And all the people in the water. Oh my goodness, look how much fun that seems!" He had his fists balled up on either side of his head by his ears, and was staring below us, transfixed.

I couldn't really say anything. When we were on the Earth, Aunt Tu had taken us to the beach and fishing a couple of times, but it was right around in Maryland, and it sure didn't look anything like this. Wow. People were laughing and running up and down the beach and playing volleyball and riding on surfboards and in small boats and it looked just like something in the movies.

I heard a whistling sound and looked at Meranda, who was just as frozen-looking as Dakota. Her lips were barely open, and the whistling sound was coming from her. "Man oh man" came softly from her mouth and I could tell that she was as blown away as we were. Even more, probably, cuz at least we had seen some stuff that looked like this on TV, but M never even had a TV, she'd told us. There was no electricity in her village, so no TV. Something like this was far from what she'd ever been close to.

I finally was able to speak. "Hey, y'all what you think? Let's get closer!"

We floated down until we were actually down there with all these people, floating right above the sand, and we could feel the heat coming up from it. We could hear the ocean too, and the sound was like music. Like a rhythm. "Whoooossh" as the waves came in, then "Whhoooooo" as they went back out. It was like magic, this whole scene. "Whoooossssshh,

Whhooooo." And something about being here was making everybody happy. People were laughing and skipping and running and smiling and holding hands and just happier than I've ever seen a group of people before. It was amazing, and the three of us sat down on the sand and just took it all in.

This was nothing like how either of us had spent our time on Earth. And I was beginning to understand why Aunt Toni was always traveling to islands and places near the beach. It was a whole different ballgame, I could see.

We sat there until the sun went down, watching the people staring at the big yellow ball as it disappeared into the ocean – turning the sky red, orange, yellow and finally a little green as it left. Truly amazing!

"OK, so what now?" I heard Meranda say, as the sun left completely and folks started picking up their blankets and balls and walking away. It was weird to hear her, cuz neither one of us had said anything much for the whole time we were sitting there. It was like we all were just sucking in the scene, bringing it into our pores; it was so different, and so wonderful. Her words were like waking up after a long sleep.

"Huh?" 'Kota grunted. He really looked like he had been sleep – eyes half-closed, with that far-away look in them.

"Did I wake you?" Meranda said – looking at him with a frown. "Sorry, sir – didn't mean to disturb your rest. Come on, let's hit the road." She ran her hands through her clown-wig hair and started flapping her wings.

Dakota looked at me and words started tumbling out of his mouth "Erik, can you believe this place? Did you ever think we would be somewhere like this? This is the bomb! This is still the United States and people live like that here. Did you know that? Can you imagine spending a day in a place like this? Or a week? Or actually live here? Man!"

I was as blown-away as 'Kota was, and I knew that M was too – but all I said was "I know little brother, it's amazing. Come on, let's get going."

We started back floating, heading on to Haiti, and we were quiet again. Now that we were starting to see how other people lived, it was shocking to us, when we compared it to how we had grown up. I guess that's why books and TV and movies are so good, so you can see that there is more to life than how you are living yours. But when we see stuff like this, it feels kinda tough when your own life had been so different. And so hard.

CHAPTER ELEVEN

Even though Dakota was our master geographer – pointing us in the direction of the places we wanted to go, M had made herself the general look-out, pointing here and there as we floated along – not wanting us to miss whatever it was that she thought was interesting. With her position in the front of our upside-down V, it was perfect.

"Look. There! To the right and down. That must be Haiti!" M's hair was bobbing in her excitement and she had made a quick turn to the right, motioning for us to follow her.

We followed her and looked down. You could tell that something big had happened there. As we floated closer, I started feeling stuff that I hadn't felt over any of the other places we had floated. Suddenly I felt like crying. And I hadn't even seen anything yet. But I could feel the energies that were coming up from that land. It felt heavy. And sad. And like everything and everybody was confused and angry. And that made it look different from the air, too. Even though the sun was shining, all of the land looked dark.

"Oh my goodness," Meranda whispered. "This feels like it used to feel in my country, when the wars were going on. Heavy and sad. Listen to the crying. Oh mon dieu."

We got a little closer and could now see all of the confusion that was going on down there, and a tear escaped from my left eye. I wiped it away quickly and started turning to another direction. I didn't really want to see any more.

'Kota floated up beside me and quietly said "I wish we could tell them about all the souls we saw from Haiti on their way to Angel-Land, and let them know that they're gonna be angels and will be able to help them soon, and send them love."

"Yeah, 'Kota, they sure will."

We had learned since we'd been there that souls in Angel-Land have the power to send good feelings back to those they had left behind, and even to people they had never known on the Earth. 'Kota knew that the new souls in Angel-Land would soon be doing that for the people of Haiti, soon as they got over the shock of having left the Earth so suddenly and gotten adjusted to where they are now. Still, it was hard to see and I was ready to leave.

"C'mon, M, let's head to Jamaica."

Meranda turned around and started floating behind me and Dakota, not saying anything. She still had a stunned look in her eyes and was moving more slowly than I'd ever seen her move before. She kept looking down, and then floated up beside me and pulled on my shirt. "Look. Over there."

I looked where she pointed and there were a couple of really bright lights beaming strongly from below. I mean bright! I pointed them out to Dakota and we all floated down for a closer look. As we got closer, we saw that one of the lights was coming from a group of women on the beach. They were all dressed in white, and were singing and dancing and what sounded like praying. And whatever it was they were saying and singing sure was making them happy. Swirling all around them was this huge bright light, and the more they sang and prayed and chanted, the bigger the light was growing, and it was starting to float over to the other areas close by to where they were.

"Who are they, and what are they saying?" I whispered.

We floated even closer and watched as the women moved up and down the beach at the edge of the ocean, barefoot, with their white dresses flowing and dipping in the water. They clapped and stomped their feet to the beat of the song. Their voices sounded like a bunch of gobble-dee-gook to me, but Meranda chimed in and said "I know that song! My grandmother used to sing it to me when I was little!"

She started singing with the women, translating it from French into English for us: "Oh Dear God, our most High, please keep us near and protect us nigh. Watch over the babies and the children too, and keep them safe and close to you." Meranda's voice sounded like she was strangling on the last couple words and she stopped, turning her head away from us.

'Kota wanted to know why people all the way over in Haiti, so far away from France, were speaking and singing in the French language, and Meranda started to explain. She told us how the French, like a lot of other countries, had gone out in boats in the 17th and 18th centuries and taken over a lot of different places – islands and countries, like hers. They took over Haiti in 1697, and after lots of fighting and led by a former slave, Toussaint L'Ouverture, the French army was beat and Haiti became an independent country in 1804.

"In school, we had to learn about French history all over the world," M told us. "I really didn't care much about history and what was happening in other places, cuz there was so much going on in my own country that we didn't know about. But anyway, that's the story about Haiti. There are lots of places in the world far far away from France, that still speak French cuz of those days. Kinda weird, I think, but.."

We had gotten close to where the other bright light was coming from, and we saw that it was shining out from a building. Busting through the windows and the walls. We got closer and saw that the building was full of babies and little children.

"Wow," Meranda said, "you think they're there cuz they were lost in the earthquake?"

"Probably," I said, "and the families haven't found each other yet. I hope they do."

"Me too," 'Kota chimed in, "but look at how cute they are, and how happy they seem."

I guess because they were so little, and didn't really know what was going on, you could tell that the little babies and children were happy, and glad to be with each other. The glow from their hearts and their smiles were lighting up the whole building and starting to move outside the building and into other parts of the country, just like the lights from the women in white on the beach.

'Kota looked at the children with the biggest grin on his face and said "Wow. These little babies are changing everything around them and they don't even know it. Just by being happy and having a good heart. That's awesome!!"

CHAPTER TWELVE

Those two bright lights shining up in the middle of all that darkness in Haiti really made us feel better, and took away the awful feelings we'd had when we first looked down at that country. The feeling we had had, that it was over for them, and everybody – the children, big people, everybody - was through. Now, we knew there was hope and that surely more lights would start and spread throughout the country – bringing back some happiness down there. They sure needed it.

As we floated off, we were all pretty worn out from what we had seen. I looked at 'Kota and instead of his usual - stretched out on his side with his head propped up on his hand – the dude was laying flat on his back, eyes closed, and humming! I hadn't seen him so relaxed since we started on this traveling thing.

"Yo, Mr. Dakota! You sleeping, or what?!", I kinda yelled at him. 'Kota barely turned his head to look at me, eyes still half-closed, and grunted. Didn't even answer. Just grunted, grinned, and turned his head back around and started humming again.

Meranda usually traveled laying flat on her stomach, eyes wide open and head turning constantly, looking at every little thing that we floated over. She alerted us to every ant that moved and every leaf that twisted for a nano-second in another direction. We called her Hawk-Eye behind her back, but really appreciated her looking out. Even Meranda was chillin' now.

"Cher, arête!" Meranda said to me. She was always trying to be our mother, even though she was only 12 – a year older than me and two years older than Dakota. And please stop speaking French to us! She knows we don't know that language. But before I could tell her what I was thinking – in English, mind you – there was the loudest sound I have ever heard.

"Ka-Boom!!"

It sounded like a gazillion twenty-story brick buildings crashing down. All at once. So loud that all the birds that had been flying around us took off in another direction.

"What was that!?" Dakota yelled, sitting straight up.

Meranda's eyes got wide and her mouth flew open. I couldn't say anything – just felt this huge lump in my stomach and my heart started beating real fast. I opened my mouth to try to say something but just these little scratchy sounds came out.

We looked at each other and then looked down. This black, thick, smelly smoke was coming up from the Earth. It smelled twenty times worse than the garbage trucks that used to come through our neighborhood. Meranda started gagging and if we weren't angels, I'm sure she would've thrown up.

A great big hole had opened up in the Earth and the stinky smoke was gushing up out of it. Like I can imagine a volcano must look when it is erupting. And even though I couldn't believe what I was seeing, a dog was flying out of the hole. With a green bandana tied around his neck – barking his head off. Right behind him, with his right arm raised up in a fist, was a boy. A boy. And a dog. Coming out of the ground. Now, all of our eyes looked like they were gonna' pop outta' our heads. I know mine felt like it. We couldn't speak. Just looked at each other and then back at the boy and the dog.

Somehow, I knew this was gonna' be wild.

They didn't give us a chance to catch our breath. This boy, and the dog with the green scarf around his neck, flew right to us - black stinky smoke billowing around them as they came.

"What tha?" I balled up my fists and got ready for whatever was coming, cuz it didn't look good. Out the corner of my eye, I could see Meranda's blond hair bobbing and I knew she was getting ready too. I could feel Dakota close to my back, just where I wanted him to be. I was still the big brother, and I didn't know what was getting ready to go down.

"Hey!" I yelled. "Stop right there! Who are you and what do you want?" The whole time since we had left Angel-Land, we hadn't come across any other beings that had come close to us. We saw a lot of angels floating around as we traveled, and they would wave, and we would send greetings to them by thought, but they always kept going and never got too close. It had just been us, really, this whole time, and now this clown and his dog were coming right at us, full speed ahead.

"I said stop. Right now."

My voice must've been serious, cuz they both stopped in their tracks, with the dog looking up at the boy like "do I really have to?"

The boy put his hand on the dog's neck and said, "Hey. Who're you all and what are you doing around here? What year is it?"

"What year?!", Meranda shouted."Who are you and why do you want to know what year it is? And how did you come out of the ground like that?" Meranda had gotten herself together, had her hands on her hips, and was demanding answers. The blond hair was going crazy – like it had a life of its own.

The dog started a low growl and the boy patted him on the head. "My name is Stix and this is my dog, Chief Braxton.

We've been living underground for a long time, in a place called Toxburg."

"What? Underground?" Even Dakota was coming around now and getting closer to this strange-looking pair. "How can you live underground?"

"I don't know. We just did. For a long time. There're a lot of people under there."

"So what're you doing out here now?" I asked. I still had my fists balled up cuz I didn't like this guy. Or his dog. Didn't like them one bit.

"I guess there was an aftershock from the earthquake. Me and Chief Braxton went for a long walk today and just as we were turning around to go back home, we heard this loud noise and looked up and that hole opened up in the ground. We just flew up it. You saw us. We're free now. And we're not going back."

Chief Braxton howled a long, high-pitched yelp. He seemed to be confirming what his master was saying.

This was really too much for me to handle. Living underground??! I was just getting used to living in Angel-Land, and now to traveling and seeing some more of the world. And now this nut was telling me he lived under the ground? Geeeeezus! What next?

"So." Meranda had moved closer to the boy and Chief Braxton (who names their dog Chief Braxton?) and was staring down at them. He looked like he was about 14, but M was still taller than he was. She had a really intimidating look on her face and her hands were still on her hips. Fists still balled up. "You're saying you don't know how long you were down there. Where is your family? Are they down there too? Did you ever live on the Earth, before you went under it? I mean, come on. Really?" She gave them a look that could've scared rain frozen, on its way down to the ground. Scared me, and she was my friend.

"Hey. I'm just telling you what it is. Yeah, I used to live on the Earth, a long time ago, and I died. OK? Me and my dog were someplace we weren't supposed to be and something happened and we died. And next thing I knew we were in this smelly, dark place, with a lot of other people, and they told us it was called Toxburg, and we've been there ever since."

"But where are your mother and father?" Dakota wanted to know. "And your friends, and sisters and brothers?" 'Kota always, just always, took the soft approach. He looked, now, like he might want to hug this weird-looking boy, just because he didn't have his family.

"I don't know where they are. Haven't seen them since I left the Earth. That's why I wanted to know what year it is – so I can figure out if they'd still be living, or what."

I was still looking this character up and down, and keeping an eye on the dog. I usually love animals, but I didn't like the way this one looked. "We don't know what year it is either. We left Earth too, but we live in a place called Angel-Land, near the birds and the clouds. See these wings? That's what we got when we moved there."

Stix now looked me up and down. "Oh, yeah… we've heard about that place. That's where everybody is all sweet and nice, right? And help out the people that're still on the Earth, huh?" He made a sound like a snort. "Well… that ain't what we do in Toxburg, that's for sure."

I really didn't like him now. "OK, well, nice meeting you all. We're on our way someplace so we've gotta go. Good luck." I looked at Meranda and Dakota. "Come on, y'all. Let's hit it."

We turned, and started flying away from that bizarre pair, and floated awhile before anybody said anything. I knew that M and 'Kota were in as much shock as I was. Oh my God! A frikkin' boy and a dog who lived under the ground?! And there were lots of other people living under there too? Shut the front door!

Dakota broke the silence. "Erik, do you think he can hear us talk? What was that, Erik? Did we really talk to a boy who lived under the Earth?"

We all stopped, mid-air, and looked at each other. "Hey man, I don't know what that was. I know I didn't like it. Didn't like him or his dog. And I want to get as far away from them as possible."

"Me too," M chimed in. Her hair, for the first time ever I think, wasn't moving at all. I think it was in shock too. "When I was growing up in my village, I used to hear stories about people who lived underground, and they weren't good stories. I never thought they were true."

"Come on. Let's just get to Jamaica. I know it'll be fun there." Between Haiti and Stix and his dog, we had seen enough. I started floating again, and Meranda and Dakota were right behind.

CHAPTER THIRTEEN

We didn't have far to go to get to Jamaica, as the distance between there and Haiti is only about 120 miles. Aside from loving Bob Marley, me and Dakota were really excited to go to Jamaica because Aunt Toni used to live there and used to tell us about how beautiful it was and how much she loved the Jamaican people.

Aunt Toni met her husband in Maryland, when they were both jogging in Sligo Creek Park. He was from Jamaica and later on they got married and moved back there. That was a long time before me and 'Kota were born, but our mom got to visit them there when she was just a little older than we were when we left Earth – about 13, I think. It was one of the things she talked about a lot and when she and Aunt Toni got together, they always talked about how good the food was, and what a good time they had had. We've seen pictures of them, climbing up Dunn's River Falls, with everybody holding hands as they went up this really high waterfall, stepping on the rocks that led up to the top. Mama said it was really slippery, and that she and Aunt Sylvia, who went up too, kept laughing and screaming all at the same time. White Grandma went on the trip too, but she didn't go up the falls. She had a hard time walking sometimes anyway cuz her legs got tired a lot, and she didn't like swimming, so no way José on the falls.

Aunt Toni and her husband lived in Port Antonio, on the east side of the island, so we floated over there first.

"Zowee!" 'Kota yelled out, as we crossed from the ocean to the land. "Man that's pretty!"

Meranda was excited too. "Nothing but mountains and trees and flowers and rivers! Wow this is gorgeous."

You could tell that it rained a lot cuz everything was so green, and shimmery-like.

Of course, Smarty-Pants 'Kota knew some stuff about the country. "They grow a lot of coffee in the mountains on this side. See, look there, those are coffee trees."

How that boy knows so much about stuff amazes me. I guess if you read a lot like him you get to know stuff.

"And look at those trees, full of mangoes and bananas and oranges. And those pineapples over there on the ground. Reminds me of my country," M told us. "You talk about some good eating! Oooh, my mouth is watering just thinking about it. Sure wish we could still eat stuff."

I was just thinking the same thing. This was one of those times when I wished I could still taste stuff from the Earth, cuz everything looked so good. I saw a little boy about four years old eating a mango and there was this orange juice from it dripping all down his chin and he kept sucking on the mango and licking his fingers from the juice. It looked better than any McDonald's hamburger and french fries I'd ever had and I used to love me some Mickey Dee's food!

There was a different kinda feeling floating over Jamaica too. Like, more vibrant and energetic than floating over the ocean. And different from DC too. "Hey y'all. Doesn't it feel different here than anyplace else we've been?", I asked my two buds.

'Kota and Meranda stopped looking all around and I could see they were trying to feel what I was talking about.

"Hmmmm" Meranda said. "Different how?"

"I don't know. Like, even though there's no sound up this high, and there're not a lot of people in the mountains, it feels, like, exciting. Like there's something going on here that feels good."

"Well it sure feels better here than over Haiti, I know that," 'Kota said. "Just looking at this beautiful place makes me feel good."

"Hey 'Kota – remember how we used to dance whenever we heard Jamaican music? Oh man! You shoulda seen us, M. If some reggae music came on the radio, 'Kota and I would start hopping around like crazy! It just made us want to move!" I looked at Dakota and we both started our reggae hop. Right there above the mango and coffee trees.

"What? You think you all were the only ones to love reggae music?" Meranda started hopping too and we all danced and laughed until tears were coming out of our eyes.

Aunt Toni used to tell us that she thought the people of Jamaica were special. And unique. She was told while she was living there that when the slave ships brought captured Africans to the Caribbean and the Americas, Jamaica was one of the first places they landed. The ships' captains put the slaves who had given them the most trouble on the long and awful ride over, off the ship first, in Jamaica. These were the men and women that seemed to have the most highly spirited natures; and they had refused to buckle down and act like slaves. They had been tricked or forced to get on the ship, and were taken away from their homes – and they were not giving in easily. They fought, bit, starved themselves and even jumped overboard, to avoid becoming slaves. When they were forced to stay on the ship and kept from jumping off, they made life miserable for the slave sellers.

Legend has it that when the first slave ships landed on the waters near Jamaica, the unruly ones were put off the boat there, so they wouldn't have to deal with them anymore. A lot of them ran into the mountains, and became known as the Maroons. There are still Maroon communities in Jamaica today. Aunt Toni thought that this strong energy that the early Jamaicans showed was still in them. They were proud and passionate and showed their spicy spirits in their food, their music and their politics.

Floating over Jamaica, our little gang of three also got to see how awesomely beautiful this island country was. Wow! The mountains, like the Blue Mountains and the John Crow Mountains, and the more than 100 rivers with the Black River being the longest one - and gushing waterfalls everywhere, were unlike anything we'd ever seen before.

It sure wasn't like DC's scenery. I asked Meranda if there were any rivers in the Congo, where she was from.

"The Congo River is the second longest river in all of Africa! It's huge. And there are lots of mountains there too. My country is the second largest country in all of Africa" she proudly told us. "I didn't get to see a lot of it, but we were taught about it in school."

It was pretty awesome to think that the lands all over the world were so different.

Floating like this, over this beautiful country, made us all feel great. We kept being passed by all kinds of birds in lots of different colors, and Mr. Dakota told us that there were over 300 kinds of birds there! The flowers were off the chain!

It was starting to get dark, and when we floated over this sweet little river, Meranda suggested we go down and settle there for the night.

"Sounds good to me," 'Kota said. "I'm getting kinda tired of moving."

I admitted that I was too. "Yeah, boy, it's been quite a day, huh? We can set off and see some more tomorrow."

We floated leisurely down to the grassy area beside the river, passing some more of those luscious-looking mango trees on the way down. Man, if only I could taste one…

CHAPTER FOURTEEN

"What was that? Y'all hear something?" I turned to look at Meranda and Dakota and they had stopped too, and were leaning toward what sounded like someone crying.

"Where's that coming from?" Dakota asked.

"Shhhhh." Meranda put her finger up to her mouth. "I think it's over there. Near those trees."

We floated over toward the orange trees and the sound got louder. It was somebody crying!

"Look," M said "on the ground. Right there."

We all looked and there was a little boy, about six or seven, laying on his back under one of the orange trees, crying his heart out. A large sack, and a whole lotta' oranges, were spread out all around him.

"He must've fallen," 'Kota whispered, "when he was picking oranges."

"So you figured that out, huh Mr. Smarty-Pants. Brilliant deduction." I couldn't help teasing my dear little brother whenever I could.

He just looked at me and rolled his eyes. "Do you think we can help him?"

The little boy had stopped crying and was looking, wide-eyed, at where we were floating right above him.

"Oh my God do you think he can hear us?" Meranda asked, real quietly.

"Of course I can hear you. I can see you too," the little boy answered. "Can you help me please? I was climbing this tree, trying to take some oranges home for my family, and I fell off of one of the branches. I can't move my legs."

"But how can he hear us?" M went on whispering. "That can't be."

"But I can hear you. Can you just help me please? My leg hurts and I have to get home before it gets dark. My mother doesn't know where I am."

We looked at each other. This little boy was seeing and hearing us, and he needed help. How could he see us? Except for people looking in our direction like they thought maybe they felt something, nobody on Earth had actually seen or talked to us since we were angels.

"Do you think we can lift him? Where does it hurt little fella?" Meranda asked him, floating down right beside him.

"Right here. This leg." The little boy touched above his knee on his right leg.

"It's swollen," M said, "and it's bleeding. Can you feel this?" Meranda lightly touched the little guy. 'Kota and I looked at each other. I was wondering if he was gonna be able to feel an angel touch.

"Oww. Yes I can feel it. That hurts!"

"I'm sorry. Hmmmm… what do you think guys? How're we gonna' move him? We have to help. If we go and try to tell his mother, she might not be able to see us. Oh Lord."

I had an idea. "Let's wrap some of these branches together and lay him on them, like a little cot, then float him to his house. Little guy, can you show us where you live?"

"Of course! I know where I live! Just please help me get there."

Dakota and I got to working on the branches. It was weird, being able to handle them. Other than ringing Aunt Toni's doorbell, none of us had tried doing anything physical on the Earth since we'd been angels. I didn't know we could! Wow! This was cool.

"OK, now get some of that long grass, 'Kota, and we can wrap it around these branches."

We worked for awhile and got a nice little pallet together while Meranda stayed close to little Teddy. He had calmed down now that he saw we were gonna help him. M had opened up his pant leg where it was torn, made a little bandage from the material and pressed it down on the bleeding. Coming from her country village where there weren't any drugstores, she was used to seeing her mother work with herbs and whatever natural things were around when somebody got sick or hurt.

"Why do you all have wings?" Teddy asked, as we brought the pallet back and were trying to figure out how to get him on it. "Are they real? Are you angels?"

"Yes, we're angels," Meranda told him, "and you're the first person that's been able to see us."

"Maybe because I needed you to help me, I can see you."

"May be" I said. "May be." I was still blown away that he could.

With all three of us working, we were able to slide Teddy onto the pallet, and we put our arms under it and started floating up.

"It's working!" 'Kota shouted. "Yea!" His eyes were as big as basketballs and his eyelashes were fluttering like crazy. Meranda had the biggest grin on her face that I had seen yet. I was pretty psyched too.

"That way," Teddy pointed. "My house is on the other side of that field."

We got into a rhythm, and were floating off in the direction Teddy had pointed, when I started hearing a dog bark. I looked down to see where it was coming from, then realized that the barking was getting closer, and sounded like it was coming from the air, and not the ground. M and 'Kota started looking around too and I think we all saw it at the same time. Stix and Chief Braxton were flying toward us at mega-speed – Chief Braxton's bandana streaming behind him and Stix with his arm raised, and the weirdest smile on his face.

Teddy started screaming. Meranda tried to calm him down and all that movement was making it hard to keep the pallet steady. Dakota looked more scared than I'd ever seen him before and I knew I had to take over.

"What do you want Stix and why have you followed us?" I was trying hard to keep the nervousness out of my voice. I did not like that this boy and his stupid dog were here again. How did they find us and why was this fool dog barking his crazy head off?

Stix just laughed.

I turned to 'Kota and Meranda. "Come on, let's keep going." Teddy's face had gone white and it looked like it was hard for him to breathe. M was rubbing his arm and hand, and saying something soothing to him. The blond clown-wig hair was slowly moving back and forth.

"Where're y'all going?" Stix asked, with a snicker. "Can I help?"

"We're going to take this little boy home," I said. "And no thanks – we've got it."

What happened next was so sudden that I can't really say I know what went down. All I know is that stuff and angels and dog fur were all flying in every direction at the same time, and I was tumbling feet over head. When I was able to right myself I saw little Teddy - diving toward the ground. Head first. I started flapping my wings as fast as I could, heading for him. I caught a glimpse of blond hair outta the corner of my eye as I dove, and knew that Meranda was heading for him too. We got to him about six inches before his head crashed onto the ground. M and I grabbed him just as I heard Dakota yelling my name.

"Erik! Help!"

We looked up and saw Dakota – my little brother - hanging upside down from one of the orange trees, his wings wedged in between the branches.

Stix's horrible laughter was booming from the air – as he and Chief Braxton went flying away to the north. "Stop trying to be such goody two-shoes" he yelled. "See you next time, my little angels. Hahahaaaaaaa Haaa!"

CHAPTER FIFTEEN

M and I rescued the pallet and got Teddy stable on it again. "Hold on, 'Kota," I yelled up to him. "We're coming."

We laid Teddy and the pallet on the ground, and flew back up towards Dakota, who had tears streaming down his face. "Erik get me down, please! How did he do this to me?"

"It's OK, Buddy, we're here. We're gonna' get you down."

Meranda and I looked at each other and I was sure that my face looked as angry as hers did. How in the world did that creep find us and why did he do this?!

"OK, 'Kota – we've got you," Meranda said. "Move a little to your left, and I'll unhook you from this side."

M and I worked carefully, not wanting to hurt Dakota as we untangled him. Somehow, that horrible Stix had wedged him really good in between the branches.

"Alright little brother. Here we go. Move your right leg a little bit towards me and I'll grab it. That's it. I've got you."

Finally, we got Dakota and his wings outta' the tree and I hugged him up really good. Meranda grabbed him next and squeezed him. "Come on little fella. You're OK," she said.

Dakota just looked at us both, and didn't say a word. I could tell he was kinda in shock. I mean, 'Kota is like the sweetest kid in the world, and it burned me up that somebody would mess with him. If I could get to that Stix.. But we still had to get Teddy home.

I grabbed 'Kota around the shoulders and floated with him back down to where we'd left Teddy. That little guy was totally freaked out by then. It was one thing to see and be rescued by three angel children, but to then have that Stix and Chief Braxton come outta' nowhere and flip us all around like that – I guess his head would be spinning. I still hadn't figured out how Teddy could see all of us anyway.

"Hey, Teddy, we're back," Meranda told him, "and we're gonna' get you home. Don't worry."

Teddy was sniffling and snot was running outta' his nose. "Who and what was that?!" he managed to get out. "And why did they flip me like that? I thought I was gonna' hit the ground and bust my head open!"

"He's an awful guy that we saw on our way here, who used to live under the ground. He must have followed us here," Meranda told him. "Don't know why he was so mean to us, but he's gone now. Come on. We've got you. Alright boys, lift!"

We lifted the pallet with Teddy on it and started back toward the field. I kept looking around as we floated, making sure no more surprises from Stix and Chief Braxton were heading our way. I started singing, too, hoping that that would calm everybody down a little bit.

"Don't worry, about a thing, cuz-a every little thing, is gonna' be alright", I sang. "Saying don't worry…" Everybody knew Bob Marley's song, and they all chimed in. Me and 'Kota from DC, Meranda from the Congo, and Teddy from Jamaica, and we had all grown up hearing that song. It was kinda cool.

Just as the song was ending, we cleared the field and Teddy pointed down to a little house with a tin roof and a wide front porch. A woman was standing on the porch with an apron around her waist and a wooden spoon in her hand. She was looking all around, like she was looking for something. Or somebody. Teddy started whispering.

"That's my mother. She must be looking for me. Go around back."

I was thinking the same thing he must've been thinking. We couldn't float Teddy down on his pallet in front of his mother! She couldn't see us, so here would come this pallet floating outta' the sky with her son on it! She would'a had a heart attack or something! The thought of it was kinda funny, though – a boy on a floating pallet! Hahahaaaa ha

"OK y'all," I said to 'Kota and M, "let's head out this way, then turn around and head for the back of the house."

When we got around back, we floated Teddy down to the little deck right outside the back door. We helped him sit up and Meranda took a look at his leg.

"It'll be alright little guy. Your mom will take care of it from here. It was nice to meet you."

"Hey, thanks y'all! It was nice to meet you too. I've been seeing angels ever since I was really small, but I've never seen any up close like this. Come back and see me if you're ever around this way again."

"We will," I told Teddy. "Now you take care of yourself, OK? Be careful in those trees!"

It was dark by then and we were all exhausted. Poor 'Kota hadn't said much at all since we got him outta' the tree. "Let's go find a place to chill for the night," I said. "I'm beat."

We floated over to a little cave-like area on the side of the mountain. It looked like a good place to rest for the night, and it was hard to see it from the sky or the ground. I was still a little shaken by Stix showing up and I didn't want him to find us again.

"You all go on in, and I'll sit out here for awhile and keep watch. Make sure everything's OK."

"I'll sit with you, Erik," 'Kota said. "I'm not tired."

"No, you go get some rest, with Meranda. I'll come in in a little while."

They went in and I stretched out on a wide, flat rock. I think we were all asleep in two nanoseconds.

CHAPTER SIXTEEN

I woke up the next morning to Meranda stretching her arms, fluffing out her wings and running her hands through the blond clown-wig of hair. The sun was just coming up and there was a mist rising up around the mountains.

"I thought you were coming in," she said to me. "You fell asleep, didn't you?"

I rubbed my eyes and started standing up. "I guess I did. Wow. Must've been tired. Well, nobody bothered us. Hopefully they're long gone."

'Kota stuck his head outta the cave entrance and said "good morning y'all! Everybody ready for a Jamaican adventure today?"

I was happy to see that the sleep must've done him good. He came all the way out and we all high-fived. Everything was OK.

"Yeah mon," I said, like the Jamaicans, "let's hit it!" I wasn't ready to talk about yesterday and it seemed that neither of them was, either. Maybe it was a bad dream?

We had floated in to Jamaica from the eastern side, near Portland, and decided now to head west – toward Ocho Rios (which means eight rivers in Spanish, Mr. Smarty-Pants 'Kota informed us), Montego Bay and Negril. Meranda said she had even heard about Negril in the Congo – with its seven miles of white, sandy beach. Ooooh, couldn't wait to see that!

We floated along over the awesome country, looking down on small villages in the hills, lots of rivers, plenty of trees, and a ton of beautiful flowers. We saw people walking cows, riding bikes, working in their gardens and picking fruit. There were lots of little towns, too, and some areas had hotels and resort-looking places. People were playing on golf courses, and in just about every village or town that we passed, somebody was on a field playing soccer. We saw another game being played, too, where they were swinging a wide flat bat and Dakota thought that game was called cricket. I never saw it before.

We passed a lot of animals, too; like frogs and lizards and turtles. Crocodiles and even bats. There aren't too many snakes there, cuz the mongoose, which looks something like a weasel, was brought in from India to kill rats, and killed a lot of other things too. M knew some of the history of Jamaica too, and told us that it used to belong to England, until 1962 when it got its independence, and that the government is still attached to England by a representative of the Queen of England.

Everywhere we floated over this beautiful island we caught the jamming reggae music. 'Kota and M kept laughing at me 'cuz I just couldn't keep still when I heard it! As much as I love to dance, there was no way I could stop dancing to the reggae beat we heard all around us. Flapping my angel wings and hopping from side to side, I was having a ball!

Listening in on some conversations people were having, we learned that reggae started, actually, from ska, which was Jamaican music that started in the late 1950s. Everybody hears a lot about Bob Marley, but the whole country is filled with really cool singers and dancers. And boy do the Jamaicans love to party! Old and young – grandparents, babies and everybody in between, come to their parties. And dance dance dance. And since the weather was so nice and warm, all the parties can be held outside.

We floated around Jamaica for quite a while – stopping for a few days in places that we liked, and heading in whatever direction we felt like, whenever we felt it. We were really digging this cool colorful country.

One day we went cruising over the capital, Kingston, a big crowded city. It didn't look like the rest of the country, and we all agreed to hurry over it and head quickly back out to where it was much fewer cars and people.

We were floating over this shopping center as we were leaving Kingston, and 'Kota pulled on the bottom of my tee-shirt. He pointed, and I saw a little girl who was standing at the entrance to the shopping center, right where the cars were pulling in. She had one thumb in her mouth and was sticking the other hand out as the cars passed by, like asking them for something. I tugged on Meranda's shirt and pointed for her to look too and we all floated down to the little girl. She must have been about five, and I thought about our little sister, who would have been about five by then as well. Her little dress was torn and her hair looked like it hadn't been combed in a very long time.

"Hey, little girl." Meranda reached out to touch her and we could tell that she couldn't see us and didn't know we were there.

"Oh my goodness," 'Kota said. "Is she begging for money? She looks hungry. Where are her parents? She's too little to be out here by herself!"

"Yeah, I think that's what she's trying to do," I said. "But she's so little the cars can't see her. Oh goodness."

An idea came to me and I told Meranda and 'Kota what I was thinking. We high-fived. Meranda stayed there with the little girl while me and Dakota floated into the restaurant that was right behind us. Luckily, nobody was in the kitchen. We helped ourselves to some paper plates, and piled them up with food. I could see now what Mama had meant about the Jamaican food! Ooooh la la it looked good! And smelled so yummy! We found a bag and put the food in it and floated it back out to where M and the little girl were, laughing our heads off. Good thing nobody saw the food being lifted up, cuz a lotta people in Jamaica believe in 'duppies' or ghosts, so we would've scared them silly!

Meranda started laughing when she saw us, and we sat the bag down on the ground next to the little girl. She saw it, and turned her head all around, frowning. When she didn't see anybody, she opened up the sack. Her eyes got round and she started jumping up and down. There was enough food in there to feed a family for at least a few days. She looked around again and not seeing anybody close, grabbed the bag up in her arms and started running. Me, 'Kota and Meranda high-fived again and started floating out of Kingston.

CHAPTER SEVENTEEN

It was good to get outta the city. Too many people, noise and cars for me. As we floated over the open spaces again; the beautiful trees and mountains and rivers, I realized how good it had felt to help that little girl. And to help Teddy back there when we first came into the country.

"Hey, I was thinking," I told M and 'Kota when we stopped beside a river to sit for awhile. "Maybe, since we're doing this traveling thing, we can try to help any children we come across that need us. We can start looking for them as we move around. What do you all think?"

"I think it's a great idea!" 'Kota piped up. "You really think we can, I mean, being angels and all?"

"Well, you see what we just did," I said. "And what we did with Teddy. Obviously we can move some stuff around and change some stuff."

"Yeah," M said, "and I'm sure if we start looking, there're a lot of children that need us. Look at us when we were on the Earth. We all sure could've used some help from an angel. Or from somebody. Let's do it!"

We all hopped up and started dancing around, making up our dancing tunes in our own heads. Arms were waving, feet were stomping and the blond clown-wig hair was doing its own thing. That reminded me.

"Hey, M, tell me something. How did you wind up with yellow hair, coming from Africa? I thought Africans had dark hair. Did your mother have hair like that?"

Meranda's face got all frowny-looking and she poked her mouth out at me. She looked like she wanted to hit me and her left hand flew up to touch her hair. But before she could say anything, her face relaxed and she smiled. "No, she had dark hair, just like everybody else in my family and in the village. I was the only one, and everybody always looked at me and asked me about my hair."

"Hey," Dakota said, "our cousin Raven is the same way. She has this golden orangey kinda hair and nobody else in our family had it either. Mama said it's something about the genes we all have, that make us who we are. Sometimes they go back to our ancestors and we get stuff from them that nobody else has in the family now."

"Yeah," Meranda said, "that's what my mother said too. But it was still kinda weird, being the only one in the village like that. But then I started liking it. And I love my hair now!" she shouted. She put both of her hands on her head and started prancing around, pushing her hair up and down, like she was modeling it. 'Kota and I started rolling around on the ground, laughing.

"I must be special," M said, laughing. "At least that's what my father always told me. That God had made me special, and different, and that's why I have this hair."

And that was it! We decided right then that we would be kinda like angel superboy or supergirl, and try to help any kids that we saw in trouble as we were traveling. If we could. Meranda was right. Me and 'Kota sure could've used some help when we were on the Earth. Lots of children can. It felt good.

"Come on," Meranda said, "I smell something good. Let's go look."

We floated up from the river bank and followed M, who was following her nose. Pretty soon, what looked like a small village appeared below us. It wasn't big, but there were quite a few houses and what looked like a small school on the other side of the river. There was a big bunch of people in the school yard and it looked like some kind of picnic or celebration. This was certainly where the smell was coming from. We floated down closer and watched as these kids, about our age, were playing soccer. Girls were playing too, and some of the younger children were playing what looked like tag. Touching each other than running away, laughing and screaming and having a good time. The adults were either setting up the long tables with white table cloths, or standing around barbeque grills, cooking. Some of the older men were sitting on big cans turned upside down, laughing and watching the children play.

And the food! Oh my goodness. Even though we couldn't taste any of it – we could sure see how good it looked and smell that aroma. Yikes! We floated around and watched for a while. When the tables finally got set up and they put the food on them, everybody dived into it. I could understand what Mama meant now, and her love for the food here in Jamaica.

There was jerk chicken, jerk pork and jerk goat; fricasseed chicken – which is chicken with lots of onions, garlic, ketchup and soy sauce; big pans of rice and peas; fish, cooked in a bunch of different ways – fried, curried and something called escoveitched; we saw the roti that Mama used to get in DC; and there were big pots of something called 'run-down', which smelled sooooooo good, and seemed to have coconut milk and curry in it. There were pans filled with cabbage that looked yummy, big banana-looking things they were calling plantain, fried 'til they were a little black on the edges and round basketball-looking things with hard bumpy shells they were calling 'breadfruit' – that they split open and sliced up with butter. Oh man these people could cook!

"Good googa-mooga," 'Kota said. He always did love to eat. Read and eat. Eat and read. Most of the time he did both at the same time. But the boy stayed skinny no matter how much he ate!

Meranda looked like she couldn't say anything. Just stared at the food.

My mouth was watering. "Aw man" I finally got out. "Do y'all see that?!"

"That stuff looks just like the food my family used to cook!" Meranda said. "I mean the same things, I can't believe it!"

"Well, you all probably grow a lot of the same fruits and vegetables as they grow here, huh?" 'Kota asked her.

"Yeah, it's about the same weather, and yes we do. But I didn't realize they would fix their stuff like ours." M had made her way down to one of the benches that the children were sitting on at the table, and was staring at every bite this little boy was putting in his mouth.

'Kota and I looked at each other and started laughing. "Hey M, remember, we're gonna' help kids, not take their food away," I yelled at her and she got this little smile on her face. I could understand, though. While we were having fun most of the time, it was hard sometimes to see stuff we used to do when we were on the Earth, or would like to try now, and not be able to. It must've been hard for Meranda to see all that food that reminded her of home.

CHAPTER EIGHTEEN

We left the school yard and all the bomb-looking food, and started floating away. Meranda was telling us the names of all the food we had seen and telling us how they cooked it in her country. Like the people we just left, M and her family cooked mostly outside, over open fires. Nobody had an oven inside their houses like we did in DC. And water didn't come out of the pipe in the sink either. She grew up having to go and collect water every day from the rivers and streams around her village. Dakota and I were amazed. We didn't know that people didn't have running water in their houses. We thought that was something that had happened a long time ago, but Meranda told us most of their village lived like that and they didn't know any different. It was just what you did.

"Wow, we must be really spoiled in America," I said. "I thought everybody lived like we do, and something like running water was everywhere."

"No," M told us. "A whole lot of places in the world live like we do. You Americans are spoiled. Driving around in your big ole' cars like kings and queens. There were only three people in our village who had cars, and they were old torn-up ones that they had to work on all the time to keep them running. They only used them once or twice a month, to go into town. They picked up stuff for everybody when they went."

'Kota's eyes got big. "What!? Three cars in the whole village?! Well how did you get around – on the subway or the bus?"

M started laughing. "What subway, Dakota? Do you think a place with mostly dirt roads would have a subway? Yeah there were buses, but they only came once a week or so. Most of the time people walk wherever they need to go. Or ride a bicycle. Most families have at least one bicycle – and they all get to use it."

"One bicycle?!" It was a lot for 'Kota to take in, and I was starting to think that maybe we Americans were spoiled for real. Even though I always thought we were kinda poor, compared to what we saw on television, I guess we weren't! I mean, we had running water, running hot water even. And lights and inside kitchens.. Wow. It makes you think. And appreciate things more.

I was still wondering about that food we saw back there that they were calling 'breadfruit'. Was it really bread, or a fruit? I asked Meranda about it and she said "I'll show you." We floated a little while more, and she beckoned for us to head down to this huge tree right below us.

"Here, this is the breadfruit tree," she said. "And these are the breadfruits."

The tree had big green shiny leaves that looked almost like hands with long fat fingers and was full of the green bumpy balls we had seen back at the picnic. They sure didn't look like fruit. Didn't look like bread either.

I touched one of the big balls and rubbed the skin. It was rough all over, and didn't feel like anything else that I had ever touched, that was a food. Floating around there in the leaves, with Dakota sticking his nose in and trying to get a smell, we looked up and saw three people walking in our direction. One of them carrying a big beige-y plastic sack and one was swinging a long machete. The one carrying the sack was about fifteen and the other two, a boy and a girl, looked like they were about ten or eleven. The youngest boy was carrying the machete; the long, wide knives we have been seeing everywhere since we got to Jamaica. When we first started seeing them, we couldn't imagine why each man, each woman, and even every child we saw over five or six, was carrying one. And then we saw why. They were so handy in this country kinda living. We saw people cutting out a path as they walked through the brush; lopping down fruit off the tree; and even holding off mean dogs that looked like they wanted to attack. These machetes were an important part of life in the country parts of Jamaica and it looked like everybody learned to use one when they were really young.

"I think they're heading for this tree," Meranda said.

"Yup," I said. I was keeping a close eye on the swinging machete. Even though everybody seemed to be really good with them, and after all I was an angel and I didn't think I could be cut, I still wasn't used to seeing such dangerous weapons up close like that.

Dakota floated up to a higher branch of the tree but me and M stayed where we were, watching to see what these guys were gonna' do. They looked at some of the breadfruit that had already fallen off the tree and were on the ground, and picked a couple of them up. I guess they weren't what they were looking for, so they dropped them back down and started looking up at the tree we were perched on.

"That one" the little girl said, pointing up and to her left, right below where I was sitting. "That one looks good."

The older boy looked at where she was pointing and must have agreed, cuz he took the machete outta' the younger boy's hand and started walking towards the ball the little girl had picked out. He pulled down on the branch that the breadfruit was on and started swinging the machete, whacking at the end of the fruit. I scampered up to a higher branch, just in case the big knife flew outta' his hand. I'm just saying.

They picked three or four of the big fruit, put them in the plastic sack and started walking away.

"Come on," M said, "let's follow them and see how they cook them up."

The kids only walked about five minutes and there was an open fire in a shallow hole that they must have started before they came to the tree. They threw more twigs and branches on it and the fire roared up in flames. They laid some long branches cross each other on top of the fire and poked the fire up. It flamed up again and they took the breadfruit outta the bag and put them on the cross-wise branches over the fire.

'Kota's eyes got big. "Wow. I've never seen anybody cook like that before. This is cool!"

"This is how we cook most of the time in my village," M said. "I think food tastes the best like this. When I've eaten stuff from people who've cooked it in the oven, it doesn't taste as good to me. This is exactly how we would cook breadfruit. You couldn't believe how good it tastes. Wow, this brings back memories."

M couldn't take her eyes off of the breadfruit, cooking over the fire. The older boy went and sat on the ground with his back against a tree. He pulled a small knife outta his pocket and started cleaning his fingernails. The two smaller children were chasing each other, back and forth, around the area.

"It's gonna' take at least an hour before it's ready," M told us. "But boy is it worth the wait!"

Me and 'Kota just floated around the area, looking around and watching the children. It was really peaceful there – all you could hear was the crackling of the fire as it danced around the breadfruit balls, and the calling of the birds. The bumpy skin of the breadfruit was starting to turn black.

"Hey" I yelled to Meranda, "it's burning, isn't it? The outside is black!"

Meranda looked down at the fire and the big balls. "Oh no... you want it to turn black. That's when you know it's cooking alright."

After a little while, the bigger boy yelled to the younger one to throw some more twigs on the fire, and went right back to cleaning his nails. The smaller guy and the little girl stopped running and looked around on the ground, finding a few more branches.

"Here." The girl handed the ones she had found to her friend and he walked toward the fire. As he walked, his foot must've slipped on some of the small rocks and dirt that were on the ground cuz the next thing I knew, instead of dropping the twigs onto the fire, his whole arm and then his whole body was falling onto the breadfruit and in to the fire.

"Billy!!" the little girl shouted. "Billy!!"

The boy sitting under the tree heard her and looked up just as Billy's whole body landed on the fire and we all heard the horrible scream that was starting to come up out of his throat.

"Agggggggghhhhhhhhhhhhhh!!"

Before the bigger boy could get himself off the ground and get to Billy, me, 'Kota and Meranda had jumped into action and were pulling him out of the fire. It happened so fast that looking back, even I was amazed. We didn't even take the time to look at each other. From wherever each of us was, floating around the fire and the trees, we headed straight to little Billy, and got there about the same time. Me and 'Kota grabbed him, pulled him outta the fire and put him on the ground. By the time we got him there, Meranda had grabbed up a wing full of dirt and was throwing it on him, putting out the flames. 'Kota and I started grabbing dirt too and we just about covered him in it. The flames didn't stand a chance.

The other boy and the little girl had stopped in their tracks and were staring at Billy, wondering how he had flown up out of the fire and how dirt had started covering him, putting the fire out. Before anybody could say anything, I looked up. M and 'Kota looked up at the same time as I did and I knew we had all heard the same thing. A dog barking. With the sound coming at us from the sky. Oh no. It could not be.

CHAPTER NINETEEN

Before we could get our wits about us, Stix and Chief Braxton had come into view and flown straight down to where we were. Stix started grabbing huge chunks of fire from the still-burning pile, and throwing them onto Billy, who was still dazed and laying on the ground. As we picked up more dirt and threw it on him, Stix threw more fire. It was crazy!

The older boy and the little girl were really in shock now. Looking back, I can't imagine how wild it must have looked to them, cuz they couldn't see us three, and they couldn't see Stix and Chief Braxton either. They just saw Billy flying onto the ground and dirt coming up outta the ground flying onto him. Now, they were also looking at fire flying out of the pit and on to little Billy too. No wonder they couldn't move. Or shut their mouths.

"Patty, do you see what I see?" the older boy stuttered. He couldn't take his eyes off of his friend, who was still dazed, and hadn't opened his eyes. "Is there dirt and fire flying onto Billy by themselves?"

Patty didn't seem to be able to answer, just moved her head once up and once down. They both started slowly walking toward the craziness, as the dirt-on, fire-on madness was continuing.

"Boy!" Meranda yelled at Stix. "What are you doing? We're trying to help this little boy. Stop! Are you crazy?"

Chief Braxton was flying in a circle around us all, barking his fool head off while Stix laughed his horrible laugh. "I'm trying to help him too. He looked a little cold, so I'm just heating him up a bit," he said, as he threw another fistful of fire on Billy. "But I guess that's enough. He looks warm now. Come on Chief Braxton, let's hit it. These guys are boring." Stix threw his right arm up in the air, with his fist balled, and he and his dog flew straight up and away from us. Before they got out of sight, Stix looked back down at us and yelled, "see ya next time boys and girl!" and laughed until we couldn't see them anymore.

Patty looked at the older boy and asked "do you hear a dog barking?"

Now it was his turn to be unable to speak. When he saw the last ball of fire that Stix had thrown he had stopped, again, in his tracks and was just staring. I felt sorry for both of them cuz I knew that this was something they would never forget, and never be able to really explain to anybody else. As for 'Kota, me and Meranda, we were in shock too, seeing Stix and Chief Braxton again, but we kept working – picking up dirt and patting it on to Billy, making sure all of the flames were gone.

We finally saw that they were and Meranda floated down real close to Billy's face and listened to his breathing. His eyes were still closed but she seemed satisfied that he was OK. She floated from his face down toward his feet, looking closely at every part of his body as she moved over it. "He seems alright," she told me and Dakota. "No serious burns. We got to the dirt quick enough to stop it going deep. Just his clothes are singed a bit."

108

Patty and the other boy had made it to Billy's side, finally, and Patty touched his hand. "Billy, Billy," she said softly, "are you OK?"

Billy's eyes fluttered and then finally opened. He looked up at Patty and the other boy for a long minute. "Wow," he kinda breathed through his lips. "I just had the weirdest dream. There were these three little angels helping me and then this other guy came along and he was throwing fire on me. And he had a dog with him! A dog with a scarf around his neck. Really weird." Billy shook his head like he could shake the weird dream out of it.

Patty and the older boy looked at each other, and then back at Billy. "Wow, Billy, that really was a weird dream," Patty said. "Do you think you can stand up?"

She and the other boy both bent down and grabbed one of Billy's arms. They helped him to his feet and he leaned on them, stumbling a little bit.

"Come on," the boy said, "let's get home." While Billy leaned on Patty, the older boy went back to the fire and threw some more dirt on it, putting out the little bit of flames and smoke that were left. He went back to the other two and took Billy's arm. With Billy shuffling between the two of them, they started back toward home. Me, 'Kota and M floated over them for a little while, watching to make sure they were OK. All three of them looked confused, and nobody said anything. I figured it was gonna take a little while before they would talk about it and try to make sense of their day. The breadfruit had been forgotten – tossed onto the ground in all of the confusion.

When we could see the house they were heading toward, and that they were almost there, I looked at M and Dakota and said "I'm outta here. I'll catch up with you guys later," and I took off. Heading straight up.

"Erik, wait! Where're you going?" I could barely hear 'Kota's voice behind me cuz I was moving fast, and I didn't stop to answer him.

"Erik! Wait!" And now Meranda was yelling too, but I didn't turn around. I kept flying, flapping my wings harder than I ever had before.

"Errrrrrriiikkkkk, wait for us." 'Kota and Meranda were gaining on me but I kept on going, fast as I could.

"Erik! Stop!" Meranda had caught up with me – yellow hair moving like it was in a hurricane. She put her hand on my shoulder and pushed down on it. I had to stop then. "Where are you going?" she panted, totally out of breath. None of us had ever moved so fast.

"I'm going to catch that guy. And his dog."

Dakota caught up with us. "But you can't, Erik. You see how crazy he is. Stop."

I broke away from Meranda's hand and started moving again. I yelled back across my right shoulder, "I can be crazy too, you know. Somebody's gotta stop him."

Meranda and Dakota each grabbed an ankle and held on tight. "You are not going to go after them," M said. "None of us are. Come on, Erik, calm down."

"Yes Erik, please," 'Kota pleaded. "You might get hurt and I couldn't take that. Please, Erik, don't go."

I could tell that Dakota was getting ready to cry and that always got to me. And I knew what he meant. If anything ever happened to him, I couldn't take it either. But that Stix! Somebody had to stop him.

"Alright. But do not let him show his face again!"

"Come on. Let's go find somewhere to rest for the night. I'm done," Meranda said.

"Me too," Dakota said. "This day has been too much."

We floated for awhile before Meranda pointed to a spot near a river, with some beautiful palm trees right there on the bank. "How about there? Let's cop a squat and chill. My head is spinning."

CHAPTER TWENTY

We floated down to a grassy spot right near the river. We could hear it rushing downstream and could smell the sweetness from the orange trees that were growing in the area. We all sat down on the grass and just stared at the water for a long time. I put my hands in the grass and it felt so good. That cool, kinda wet feeling that you don't think about much 'til it's been a long time since you've felt it, like with us.

"What is up with that crazy Stix?" M asked. "Seems like every time we try to help somebody, he shows up! What's up with that? And how does he know where we are?" Her face looked like she was in pain, and I could understand. I'm sure mine did too.

'Kota looked like he wanted to cry and was fighting hard not to. "But why?" he asked. "We're just trying to help people. Why would he and that crazy dog want to hurt them? Did you see him throwing that fire on that boy? Why would anybody be so mean?"

I wanted to put my arms around 'Kota, cuz I could see how upset he was. But I didn't. I didn't want him to think I was treating him like a little baby, especially in front of Meranda. "Hey man," I said instead, "some people are just born mean. And we don't know what that boy has been through to make him like that. I mean – what in the world was he doing living under the ground? Maybe some horrible things go on under there, and so it's made him like he is."

"Yeah, Erik, we've seen some horrible things too, but that hasn't made us mean."

"Well that's the thing," Meranda said. "Some people go through bad things and it makes them bad, too, and some people go through bad things and they become even nicer, because they want to stop the bad from happening. I guess it just depends on who you are. But man, I can't even imagine what that boy must've gone through to make him so awful. I just hope we never see him again. Or that stupid dog."

"I'm going to sleep," I said. "See y'all in the morning."

Next morning, we all decided we had had enough of Jamaica, and were ready to move on. Meeting up with Stix again had dampened all of our spirits and we were ready for something new. Jamaica had been great until then. Leaving this country, I thought that Jamaicans seemed to have a great life-style. A beautiful country, with lots of outdoor space and an ocean for kids to play in; fresh food right off the trees and in the ground; and what seemed like strong and fun people.

We had seen that it wasn't all fun and games, though. The city life had looked a little hard – with lots of traffic and some areas with kids our ages seeming to be having a hard time; selling stuff and begging for money. I guess there wasn't as much food in the city as we saw in the country parts.

That made me a little sad 'cuz one thing, we had always had something to eat. Maybe it wasn't always what we wanted to eat, but we'd had enough. Seeing kids without food was hard.

"Well, what d'ya think?" Meranda asked. "Where should we go next?"

"Hmmmmmm....". I started thinking about some of the places I had heard about or seen on TV. Several places ran through my mind, but before I could choose one and say it, 'Kota piped up.

"I know," he said, "since we're here in the Caribbean, let's go to Belize. Remember, Erik, Aunt Toni used to live there too, and loved it."

"Yeah, I remember. She used to talk about all the different cultures in that one country, and called it her country of angels, cuz she loved the people so much. Sounds good to me!"

"Country of angels, huh?" Meranda asked. "Well we definitely need to go there! That sounds like our home!"

We all laughed and started floating up to the beautiful clouds that were hovering above us.

"It's that way," 'Kota pointed, "west of Jamaica. Straight across the Caribbean Sea."

As we floated to the west coast of Jamaica, we passed over the towns of Ocho Rios and Montego Bay. We could see lots of resorts and tourists and people on golf courses and playing on the beach. We could also smell more of that awesome Jamaican food and everywhere we floated over, hear the wonderful Jamaican music.

M looked at me and laughed. "Erik is gonna miss his music. Look at him Dakota, still dancing."

Hey, I couldn't help it. When you hear music like that, you gotta move. So what I'm an angel, I still love my music!

"That's Negril. Look, the sign there" 'Kota said. "I've heard about Negril. They're supposed to have one of the most incredible beaches in the world. Let's go down."

114

It sure enough looked incredible. Miles and miles of white sand, with little hotels and shops all along it. People were on jet-skis and little boats, and looked like they were having a ball.

"Come back to Jamaica," 'Kota started singing, from the commercials we used to always hear on TV.

There was a group of about ten children on one of the beaches, digging in the sand. They were grabbing handfuls of sand and then chasing each other up and down the beach, throwing it on their friends. We floated down nearer to them and watched, laughing at their little game. Two of the girls that we were floating over started hopping up and down and pointing at us. "Look," they kept saying to their friends "it's little angels! Right there – look. Hi!"

They started waving at us. All of their friends looked, but none of them could see us. That didn't stop the two of them and they grabbed each other's hands and twirled around, laughing their heads off they were so happy.

"Little angels" they were singing, "we love you!"

We were all surprised that they could see us, and beamed our brightest smiles at them. M flapped her wings for them too, which was a really pretty sight, cuz the sun caught them and they were shimmering and glistening. It really was nice to be seen like that.

After our encounter with the girls, and with the sounds of reggae floating up from below, we all felt "Irie", a Jamaican term we heard a lot that means "cool" or "good". We were ready to move on to Belize, and flew out over Jamaica's shores, heading west over the Caribbean Sea.

CHAPTER TWENTY-ONE

Jamaica and Belize are, like, exactly across from each other on either sides of the Caribbean Sea. All we had to do was float straight and we ran right into Belize. Cuba and the Gulf of Mexico were to the north of us but between Jamaica and Belize there is nothing but big beautiful blue ocean. Or sea. 'Kota said the Caribbean was called a sea, but the Pacific and the Atlantic, I knew, were called oceans. Neither one of us knew what the difference was and why some water was sea and some oceans. Hmmm… we'll have to ask somebody about that one day.

As we floated, with Meranda pointing out dolphins and whales, jumping and spinning beneath us, I finally brought it up. We hadn't said anything more about what happened back there with the breadfruit and the fire. And my going after Stix and Chief Braxton. I think we were all still in shock, but I needed to talk about it some more. It hit me, after I flew up after them, that I felt responsible for all of us. Like, I know I was only a year apart in age from both Meranda and Dakota, but I needed to protect them. It felt like they were my responsibilities and I would do anything to make sure they were ok. If it meant facing off with Stix and Chief Braxton, or anybody or anything else, so be it.

"How about that Stix guy?, I said. "Is he crazy, or what? And why do you think he keeps turning up?"

'Kota looked at me then looked back away, real quick like. The nice smile he had had when he was looking at the whales was gone. And he looked like he didn't want to think or talk about it and had been hoping that nobody would bring it up again. Like maybe it hadn't really happened. I had seen that look before, sometimes when Mama's boyfriend had gotten angry with us, when we were back on the Earth.

Meranda's yellow clown-wig hair started bobbing up and down, and her eyes got tight and smaller. Her fists balled up and she took a few deep breaths before she could say anything. "Man! I've never seen anybody like him before! Why is he trying to hurt people? All my life, my mother used to say to us, 'we are all here to help each other. To be nice to one another,' and in my village, we had to help each other, to survive. Somebody like Stix would've been kicked out – quick!"

"Well," Dakota finally said, "when we went to that Catholic school, the nuns used to say that sometimes, some people are just bad. They don't mean to be, but there's something inside of them that causes them to do bad things. Maybe he's one of those kind of people."

"Yeah," I said, "there's lots of people that do bad things, but here we were trying to do good things, and he comes to mess that up! I don't get it."

"I don't either," M said, "and I don't like it. He'd better not show up anymore cuz I might forget that I'm a lady."

"But he's got that dog with him!" 'Kota said. "And he looks crazy too. Oh, Erik I hope we don't see him again."

"Hey little brother, let's not worry about that fool. We have left him and his dog in Jamaica and we are off to do good things in Belize!" I did a few somersaults in the air, struck a karate pose then grabbed Dakota by the ankles and flipped him over a few times. That shook him outta' thinking about Stix and we all started laughing.

I heard "heyyyyyyy" and saw Meranda's wild yellow hair going into a nose-dive as she flew straight down to the water. A school of dolphins was spinning in the sea, jumping up outta the water and diving back in, and Meranda got right in the middle of them – jumping, spinning and diving. 'Kota and I looked at each other and dove down to her. We hovered above them and watched as Meranda became a little dolphin.

"Come on, jump in," she called out to us. But we stayed where we were. I mean, I could swim like a fish, but that was in a swimming pool. 'Kota could swim too, but we'd never been in water this big, so I was just gonna' watch this time. We could tell that the dolphins could see her, cuz they were playing with her, swimming under her and splashing her with their fins. Meranda grabbed onto one of the dolphin's fins and he carried her around the water. Wow.

Dakota was about to bust his gut he was laughing so hard. It was good to see my little bro so happy. I felt good, too. Out in the middle of the ocean, or sea, or whatever it was, it was so peaceful, and so beautiful. Just the blue of the water sparkling with the sun shining on it and the white, puffy clouds gliding from one shape into another. And the birds. Wow. I hadn't thought much about birds being out here like this but I guess so. They've got all this freedom to just fly and flap as much as they like. And go wherever they feel.

"Hey 'Kota, you think you can out-fly any of these birds?"

He looked up from Meranda and the dolphins and saw a big ole hawk, wings spread, sliding around real easy-like, over a big puff of cloud. "Yeah, sure, I could take him," he said, pointing to the hawk.

I laughed. "So you think! He's just gliding now. You couldn't.." And before I could finish that thought, and tell 'Kota that there was no way he could out-fly a hawk if he was really moving, the hawk did a nose-dive, at what looked like a gazillion miles an hour, and headed straight down to the water. Before I could blink, he was heading back up to the clouds, with a huge fish in his mouth. Or beak. Or whatever it is that hawks have.

"See?" I said to Dakota. "That is exactly what I was just gonna' tell you!"

We both laughed and Meranda joined us, yellow clown-wig hair now sopping wet, and instead of being all over her head like it usually was, it was hanging down around her shoulders in wet ringlets. Kinda cute, actually. But I'd never tell her that.

"Wow," she said, "that was fun! Those dolphins are amazing! I could actually communicate with them. They do the same thing, with telepathy, that we angels do. We talked, just like they were human, or I was a dolphin. That was sooooo cool. It's like I've made some new friends!" The grin on Meranda's face was about the biggest I had ever seen. On anybody. I was happy for her.

As we floated along, we saw other angels who were out exploring too. Or going somewhere in particular. We always waved and smiled at them. We never saw any other young angels, like us, though. They all must stay in Angel-Land. I kinda miss Angel-Land, and Mama and our great grand-parents. Maybe after Belize, we should get back up there for a while.

CHAPTER TWENTY-TWO

Aunt Toni used to call Belize her "country of angels", cuz she thought the people there were so special. She lived there for almost three years in the early 1990s, before we were born. It was a really funny story how she wound up living there and me and 'Kota got some good laughs when she told it to us. We couldn't believe that she had just picked up and left DC, her job, apartment, car and cats, to go with her boyfriend to Salvador de Bahia, Brazil, which was where they were headed when they left – driving a Dodge van.

"Driving??! How were you gonna' drive to Brazil?" we asked her. "There's a lot of land and ocean between here and there! How were you gonna' do that?" We were at her house and Aunt Toni pulled out one of those big books that have colored maps of the whole world – an atlas I think they're called – and showed us how you could drive south from Washington DC, passing through Virginia and the Carolinas and all those other states, into Mexico and down through Central America. After passing the countries of Belize, Guatemala, Honduras, El Salvador, Nicaragua, Costa Rica and Panama, the Panama Canal lets you cross the ocean and go into Colombia, South America. From there, you can go into Brazil, and on to Salvador de Bahia, which is in the northeast area of Brazil, on the South Atlantic Ocean.

"Holy Moly!" Dakota had shouted. "How long're we talking here – five years to get there? I'd be an old gray-haired man if I was on that trip!" Aunt Toni had laughed and told us that the plan had been to take their time traveling through all the different countries, stopping here and there as they felt like it. Her friend was gonna' take pictures and videos and she was planning to write all about their trip.

Well – after they struggled trying to speak Spanish all through Mexico and arrived into Belize, they decided to stop. It was the first time they were able to speak English with people since they'd left the US and they thought they would hang out there for awhile. They both fell in love with Belize – which used to be called British Honduras – and the people there. After a few months in Belize, Aunt Toni got a job there and they never went any further.

"Look, that must be it!" Hawkeye Meranda had spotted land, and was pointing to what looked like a few small islands up ahead. Behind the islands was a ton of land. A long coastline that stretched out as far as we could see.

"I thought Belize was a small country," 'Kota said. "This looks like a whole continent."

"I think this is all of Central America that we're looking at," M said. "But if Belize is right across from Jamaica, it must be right around here somewhere."

"Yeah," I said, "we've kept in pretty much a straight line all the way here. Let's get down closer and see where we are, my comrades."

'Kota looked at me with the comrade comment and I knew he was remembering the same thing I was – some movie we saw on TV where this man was calling all of his friends 'comrade' and we thought it was such a funny name to call anybody. He laughed at me and started floating down to land.

From what Aunt Toni had told us, I knew that Belize was near Mexico and Guatemala, so I figured that some of the land we were seeing must'a been some of the other countries'. She told us that when she lived there, the people of Belize were always scared that they were gonna' be invaded by the country of Guatemala, which claimed that parts of Belize actually belonged to them, and they wanted more access to the sea. It caused a lot of problems between the two countries and a lot of fear. I was hoping they had worked it all out by now.

"Hey, I'm liking this," Meranda said. She had floated down to the place that looked and felt like it had the most energy coming up from it on this coast. We were right behind her.

The place was busy, but not as busy as Jamaica's big city, Kingston. Busier, though, than Jamaica's country life.

We floated all the way down to the ground and sat on a railing around the water, looking at the street and the buildings in front of us.

"This looks like it might be downtown," 'Kota said. "Look at the buildings, and the flags. And that girl has on a tee-shirt that says 'Can you Belize it'. This must be it! Yippeeeee!"

Looking around, we could see that there were all kinds of people passing by, and we heard a bunch of different languages.

"That sounds like Spanish," M said, as a group of school children passed by.

"May be. But it doesn't sound like what those two people over there are speaking," 'Kota noted.

"Sure doesn't," I said. "And there're so many different looking people, too."

"For a small country, this is pretty amazing," M said. "Everywhere I went in my country, people looked kinda the same. Look at how many different kinds of people live here."

We saw people with skin colors and hair textures all over the map, and heard them speaking English, Spanish, Garifuna, Kriol, Mayan, Chinese and several other languages as well, just in the first couple of days we were there. We found out that the population of Belize is made up of people with Spanish backgrounds, African, Mayan and a group of people called the Garifuna who are descendants of the Carib and Arawak Indians, and West Africans. From what we heard, Belizeans see themselves, with all of the different cultures and languages there, as simply Belizeans, without all the divisions some countries, like the US, make when people look different, or speak a different language.

"That would be nice, wouldn't it, Erik?" 'Kota asked me. "If we all were just Americans, no matter what we looked like?"

"That's how it is in France," Meranda said. "The Congo used to be run by France, and we still have close ties, so many Congolese have traveled to and lived in France, and it's the same there. Everybody is just considered French, they say, no matter what color they are."

"Well, there're still lots of problems, from what I see, all over the world," I said. "Else, there wouldn't be wars still. I don't get it. Adults tell us not to fight, and to talk things out, and yet they don't seem to be able to. As soon as they don't like something another person or country does, they wanna go to war. It's not right."

CHAPTER TWENTY-THREE

We left Belize City, and floated southwest to where the capital of the country, Belmopan, is. There seemed to be more of the Mayan people up there than in Belize City and we enjoyed looking at their colorful clothing. Listening in on people talking, we found out a lot about the country and the different cultures that lived there, and decided we wanted to check out the town of Dangriga. We heard that the center for the Garifuna culture was there, and they sounded so interesting!

"So check out the map over there, Meranda, and see which way Dangriga is," I said.

Meranda peeped at the map on the front of the courthouse building and found it. "It's south" she said, "and more back toward the ocean."

"I can't wait to hear their language," 'Kota said. "I heard some people saying that that group of people started a long time ago, when they were bringing slaves from Africa and one of the ships had a wreck near the island of St. Vincent. The survivors from the shipwreck hooked up with the Arawak Indians who were living on St. Vincent and they became the Garifuna. The British fought them and beat them in a war and then took them from St. Vincent to Central America, where they migrated up and down the coast. A lot of them settled in Dangriga, so they still have their language and culture from way back in those days. Wow."

"Well, little brother you have learned a lot in this traveling thing, haven't you?" I teased Dakota. "Mr. Smarty-pants is becoming even more of a smarty-pants!"

'Kota pushed me, but he was smiling. I knew he liked that I noticed his braniac qualities.

"Come on, then," M said. "Let's go check'em out!"

As we floated toward the southeast, down to Dangriga, we passed over lots of jungle, saw the rainforest, and tons of gorgeous colorful parrots and other birds. There were howler monkeys, making the weirdest noises that made us laugh, and bunches of insects. They even have snakes and jaguars! Wow!

I think I saw a jaguar when we were passing over this huge forest-like area. Something spotted moved real quick down below and I pointed it out to 'Kota and M. But Meranda didn't want to believe it was a jaguar. I think she was just afraid. "Hey. He can't bother us," I told her. "We're angels! And besides, I would kick that jaguar's booty, for real!"

M looked at me and rolled her eyes. "Yeah, sure you would King Erik. Sure."

'Kota just laughed.

"Look," he pointed. "I think those are scorpions on that branch. Remember, Erik, what Aunt Toni told us about scorpions when she was living here? They sure look creepy."

I looked at the branch 'Kota was pointing to and got the heebie-jeebies. "Yuk. Those are scorpions?" I asked. "I'd rather tackle that jaguar I saw back there then one'a them!" Those pinchers and the long curvy tail looked like they could do serious damage, even though they were probably only about five inches long.

I saw something yellow outta' the corner of my eye and looked to see Meranda and her clown-wig hair, shooting up and away from the tree with the scorpions on it, as fast as she could. "Aaaiiieeee" she was screaming. "Those things are horrible! Get away from them."

'Kota and I floated up to where she was and I reminded her that they couldn't hurt us. "We're angels!"

"Yeah, but we don't know that. Some people in my village were killed by scorpions, and every night before we went to bed we had to shake out our covers to make sure there weren't any hiding there. Ooooh. My skin crawls just thinking about them. Ooh!"

"No problem, M," I told her. "We won't go back down there. I don't like the way they look either."

Our Aunt Toni told us that when she was living in Belize and her brother, Uncle Greg, was visiting her there was a nest of scorpions living with her too. Yuk! She didn't tell Uncle Greg and his friend Jack cuz there were only two places to sleep – the bed and the sofa and the third person had to sleep on a mattress on the floor. She knew if she told them about the scorpions, they would freak out and never get to sleep. So she waited until they were packing to leave and told them to make sure to shake out their clothes before packing them and told them why. She said that they went nuts – and were so mad at her for not telling them.

"Well, it was over then", she told them, "and you would never have enjoyed your vacation if you knew!"

Belizean culture felt a lot like Jamaican culture to us. When the people spoke English, it sounded a little like the way Jamaicans spoke English. Most of the same fruits and vegetables grow there and the people in both countries eat a lot of chicken and rice and beans – except in Jamaica they call it 'rice and peas' and Belizeans call it 'rice and beans'. As we noticed when we floated over from Jamaica to Belize - the two countries are almost exactly across the water from each other. Like, if you could throw a ball from Jamaica in a straight line, it would wind up hitting Belize. I guess if you're that close on the map, there must be a lot of similar things.

We got to Dangriga and loved it! The people were so lively and we saw men making drums and fishing on canoes and women making quilts and dolls and lots of arts and crafts. And the dancing! Zowee! They called it 'Punta rock' and they got down! Hips and feet were flying and I, of course, Mr. Music himself, jumped right in! Meranda and Dakota laughed their heads off at me.

'Kota loved the language and tried speaking some of it to me and M.

"Buiti Binafi" he would say to us, which means 'good morning', and every time we did something for him, it was "seremein", 'thank you.'

"Let's leave him down here," I told Meranda, laughing. "I think he's found his home."

"I think so too," M said. "He'd probably be a good drum-maker."

We turned and started floating away from Dakota, like we were leaving him and he flew behind us yelling "Buiti fedu," which we found out later meant 'Merry Christmas'! That boy!

CHAPTER TWENTY-FOUR

As we traveled around Belize, we kept hearing people, especially tourists, talking about the Mayan ruins. Belize was first settled by the Mayan Indians over 4,000 years ago and they left behind a lot of ruins, all through Central America. These huge, steep, really tall stone structures were all built without metal tools. We decided we wanted to see some of them and picked out the site of Altun Ha, which was not too far from Belize City. We couldn't believe it when we saw them.

"No tools?" Dakota said. "So how in the world did they build them then?" he wanted to know. "They look like something I've seen on The Discovery Channel in Egypt or something. These stones are heavy!"

"And big. And the structures are tall!" M said. "Without machines or tools, how did they get to the top, carrying heavy stones?"

"I don't know," I admitted, "but they're here, and I guess they're all throughout Mexico and some other countries too. So there must've been a lot of those Mayans in this area."

"Yup," 'Kota agreed, as he started floating up one of the sides of the Altun Ha ruin. "And look, from the top up here, you can see for miles all around! This is way cool!"

Meranda and I floated up to join 'Kota and he was right. From the top of this structure, you had a clear view to almost forever, it seemed.

"I heard one of the tourist guides down there say that the Mayans used to play ball games in the areas around the ruins, like in this huge field in front of this one," M said.

"I heard that too. I also heard that they used to bury some of their royal families in the ruins," I told them.

"Royal – like kings and queens?" 'Kota asked. "They used to have kings and queens here?"

"Yeah, I guess so," I said.

"Oh my god you think there might be people in this one?" 'Kota looked kinda spooked, and I didn't know why. We were dead too. Had he forgotten that little fact?

"I don't know about dead ones," M said, "but I think I see some live people over there on the top of that ruin on the other side of the courtyard. Look."

"Can't be," I told her. "That would be too high for a person to get to. There's no where to put your feet to climb up."

"Well, some body or some thing is moving around over there. Look," she insisted.

"Yep," 'Kota agreed. "I see it too. Looks like a little kid."

"Can't be," I said again. "No kid could climb that high. It's probably a monkey. There're a lot of them around here."

Dakota grabbed my head behind both ears and twisted it to the right. "Look," he said. "Right there. You see something pink on the roof over there? It's moving and I don't think any monkeys are wearing pink."

"Oh my god!" I said. "I do!"

"I do, too," M said, and all three of us started floating off of our roof, heading in the direction of the pink something.

As we floated, we could see that the pink figure on top of the other building was waving at us. We all looked at each other. "Can she see us?" Meranda asked.

"What the?" I wanted to know. "Who is this kid?"

There were a whole heap of folks down on the field between the ruins and we had floated over all of them. Even went down onto the field among them. And none of them, we could tell, could see us, cuz they would've just walked right through us if we hadn't moved outta the way. And now here was some kid on top of the ruin, waving at us? What the heck was going on?

Dakota moved closer to me, and so did Meranda. We didn't know what we were heading in to. And the closer we got, the more waving there was. Whoever it was in the pink was jumping up and down now, waving both of her hands.

"Look, it's a little girl," M said, "and she can certainly see us."

"So I see. And I wonder how," I muttered under my breath. This did not feel quite right.

"And there's another little girl with her," 'Kota said. "It looks like she's sitting down."

Sure enough, as we floated over the edge of the ruin, we could see the one girl, about eleven or twelve, wearing a pink weaved blouse and a green skirt with about a hundred long, black, pigtails in her hair. Somebody must've spent a whole lotta time braiding! Next to her, sitting with her legs folded Indian-style on the concrete, was a smaller girl, who looked like she was about six.

"Hey, over here angels. Heyyyy," the bigger girl in pink shouted. Her blouse was woven with a lot of different threads, like the Mayan girls' and women's clothing we had seen all around Belize. They both were smiling bright white smiles and were barefoot. The smallest one had little gold hoop earrings in her ears, and her clothes were mostly white. They didn't look at all scared, like I would'a thought they should be – up this high and all by themselves. We moved in slowly.

"Hey yourself," M said, "what're you doing up here?"

"We climbed up, and got stuck. It's too hard and too steep to get back down."

"How long have you been here?" I asked, "and where are your parents?"

The two girls looked at each other and started giggling. What was so funny?

"I'm not sure how long it's been, exactly," the one in the pink blouse said. "Our parents are down there," she said, pointing to the structure we had just been on top of.

The three of us looked at each other and frowned, but didn't say anything.

"So how can you see us?" 'Kota wanted to know. "And how did you know we were angels?"

This really sent them into a fit of laughing and the spokesperson in pink answered, when she could catch her breath, "your wings, silly! Only angels have wings! We know that."

I started scratching the right side of my head, trying to think about this, and watched Meranda moving up closer to the girls, her right eyebrow raised and her mouth twisted to the side.

"So," she said, yellow hair bouncing, "you climbed up here but you can't climb back down. Do your parents know you're up here? Have they come looking for you? What have you eaten since you've been here? Are you hungry?"

I was getting tired of the giggling, which they fell into again, and was ready to move on from these silly little girls. "Ok, look," I said, "do you want us to help you get down, or what?"

Dakota was just floating there, upright, eyes wide open, and if I could'a seen inside his head, I'm sure I would've seen little wheels turning really fast, cuz that's how he looked.

The smallest girl spoke for the first time. "Yes, could you help us get down, please? I'm sure our parents are worried about us." The two of them looked at each other again and tried hard, I could tell, not to laugh. What was so blasted funny?

"Alright, we'll help you," I said. "I'm Erik, and this is Meranda and Dakota. What are your names?"

"I'm Ixtel, and my little sister is Nelli," pink-blouse said. "And we really like your wings."

"Thank you," M said. "Come on. You can ride on my back and Dakota and Erik will take Nelli."

"Ooooh, thank you!" they both said. Nelli jumped up from sitting on the roof and they started playing a hand-clapping game with each other and singing. I couldn't understand the words, and guess it was in Mayan. It sure sounded different than the songs the little girls back in our neighborhood used to sing when they were hand-clapping. But it pretty much looked like the same kinda games.

"We can go back now," Ixtel sang in English, "back home, back home."

'Kota, M and I looked at each other again. These girls were a little whack, I think we all were thinking.

"Alright, come on!" I said. "Ixtel, climb on Meranda's back and 'Kota, grab Nelli's legs and I'll take her shoulders."

We got situated and took off from the roof of the ruin and floated down to the ground.

"Ok, here we are, girls" I said when we landed. "Do you know how to get home from here?"

And here came the giggles again. "Yes, we know how," Nelli was barely able to get out. "We just live right there."

She pointed again to the largest ruin structure and the two of them started walking toward it.

"Thank you angels!" Ixtel called back over her shoulder. "Thank you so much!"

Meranda, 'Kota and I looked at each other with eyebrows raised. I'm sure they were thinking the very same thing that I was: 'where were these girls going and what were they talking about – that they lived right there?'

We turned back to look at the girls again and just as we saw them start walking up the first of the steps of the ruins, they disappeared. One second they were there, starting up the steps and while we were looking, they were no long there! Poof!

"What?!" Meranda said. "Where did they go?"

"Come on," I said, and started floating toward the steps.

"But they were right here. Just now," 'Kota said, starting up beside me. "Where are they?"

In two seconds we were right where the girls had just been, walking up the steps. And there was no trace of them.

Anywhere. A few tourists were sitting on the steps, talking, and didn't notice us and we floated right by them.

"But what could've happened? We were looking right at them!" Dakota said.

M and I looked at each other and I think the same thought hit us both at the same time.

"You think.." she started.

"Must be.." I got out.

"What?!" 'Kota said.

"I'm thinking they must be the spirits of girls who are buried in this ruin. Didn't we hear that the ruins are also burial grounds? Yep," I said, "that must be it. How else could they have gotten up on top of that building? They must've flown up there! They must be like us! That's why they were laughing so much – they were tricking us!"

"But they didn't have wings," Dakota said. "If they're angels, how come they don't have wings?"

"I dunno," Meranda said. We had all plopped down on the concrete steps, heads spinning. "Maybe," she continued, "down here, or when you're buried in one of these tombs in the ruins, you don't go to Angel-Land like we did. Maybe you just stay around here."

"Yeah, may be," I said, and that's about all I could get out. This little encounter had taken all of the wind – right outta me.

'Kota, though, had gotten excited. "Well, I mean, do you think everybody is in there now? Or what? Do you think they can fly too, like us? Did they just float through the concrete just now?" His eyes were flashing and it seemed he couldn't keep still. Was twitching his shoulders and moving his feet up and down.

"What, Dakota," M asked. "Do you wanna try to float through the concrete too, and see if you can find them?"

'Kota's eyes got really big then. "Do you think we could? Wanna try?"

"Hey, 'Kota," I said, "slow down lil bro. I don't think we should be messing around with stuff we don't know anything about. I'm thinking we should be heading outta' here."

"And I'm thinking you're right," M said.

CHAPTER TWENTY-FIVE

We floated about as far as we could away from Altun Ha. Those two girls had shaken us all up and we were ready to leave that area. But before we left Belize, we wanted to see the keys we kept hearing about.

"What is a key, anyway?" Dakota asked. "Is it like a key that you need to open a door? What do you have to open here in Belize? I don't get it. And why do people want to go to a key? How do you do that?"

"It's spelled 'caye', 'Kota," Meranda explained, "but it's pronounced like 'key'. The cayes are small islands off the coast. Like little beaches."

"Well let's go then for sure," I said. I couldn't stop thinking about those girls disappearing and thought some nice sand and watching some kids playing on the beach might take my mind off'a them.

"Alrighty then. Let's do Caye Caulker," M said. "I've heard a lot of folks talking about that one."

"Okey-dokey then. Let's do this," I said.

We floated out to the small beautiful island, which was so cool! No cars, people just drove around on golf carts, and nobody wore shoes cuz it was just white sand everywhere. Bob Marley was popular here too, and everywhere we went, we heard his music.

"Wow, this is a great place to end our Belizean visit," Meranda said. She was laying on the sand with her feet in the ocean, kicking her heels up and down when the waves came in. I hadn't seen her so relaxed this whole trip.

Kota seemed to be enjoying it too. He was floating over the people who were out in the ocean snorkeling. Then when people came off the boats with the fish and lobster they had caught, he was hanging out in the middle of them, checking out their catch.

I was sitting by a group of guys who were playing drums and singing. From time to time, when the music got to me, I would jump up and do my thing. If they could'a seen me, they would've known I was the best dancer they had ever seen. I kinda wished I could hit the drums too, but that was ok, it was just good to hear them do it.

We had decided to hit Hawaii next. Aunt Toni had lived there too, and it was her favorite place in the whole wide world. If it had anything like the ocean and scenery that Jamaica and Belize had, I could see why.

We hung out on Caye Caulker for a few days, just chilling. It was such a great place. Everybody was laid back and enjoying themselves. Nothing like the life we had had when we were on the Earth. We all talked about how we wished our friends and families could live like this sometimes, and not be always working and rushing around like crazy, like they did where we came from. And M said she wished the people in her village could have some of this too, and not have to work so hard just to live and eat. Well it certainly was a big world, we were seeing, with lots of different stuff and people in it!

"Hey, before we go to Hawaii, can we go back to Angel-Land, to see Mama and them?" 'Kota asked.

I shrugged my shoulders and looked at Meranda.

"I don't care," she said. "It's not like we have to rush or anything. I don't mind. I might hook up with my choir and do a little singing if we go."

"Ok," I said. "But I don't wanna stay too long up there. I am really enjoying this moving around business."

"Me too," 'Kota said. "I'm just missing Mama a little bit."

"Cool. Let's go then. Let's leave tomorrow."

We enjoyed our last evening and night on Caye Caulker, which just happened to be a night with a big beach party. Man was that fun! The dancing and the music and all that food! The smells of that lobster and fish cooking 'bout slayed me. My eyes enjoyed it even if I couldn't taste it, and I danced the night away.

The next morning when I woke up, Meranda was standing at the edge of the water, flapping her wings and looking out over the sea. "I just saw a whale breaching," she said. "What an awesome sight."

"Wow, I wish I could've seen that. We've seen some pretty incredible things on this journey, haven't we?"

"Yep. Sure have. I never would've thought there was so much out here in the world, and we've only seen a little piece of it so far."

"You're right. This is amazing. I can see now why Aunt Toni was always traveling. There's a lot to see. It'll be good to see Mama again, too, and we can peep down over DC and see all our family there."

'Kota walked up, rubbing his eyes.

"Sleep good, lil bro?" I asked him. "It's nice out here, isn't it?"

He nodded his head up and down. "Yep. This has been nice. I could stay here a long time, but I'm ready whenever you all are. There's still lots more to see."

"Alrighty then! So long Belize, and thank you," I said.

"You mean 'seremein' don't you?" Dakota asked, using his Garifuna words.

M and I cracked up, and I wondered how long he would remember his new language. Knowing him, though, forever.

We headed straight up and then out to the north, thinking we would go back in the other direction, over Mexico and then the southern part of the United States. This was gonna' be good.

As we passed over the Yucatan Peninsula of Mexico, we floated over the Gulf of Mexico, another big body of water at the southern part of the United States and to the east of Mexico. We realized we were heading in the direction of New Orleans, Louisiana.

"Oh!" Meranda said, "I have always wanted to see New Orleans. They speak a kinda French there called Creole, cuz the French did a little settling there a long time ago too."

"Yeah, I've heard a little about New Orleans, too," I said. "That's where they have Mardi Gras and a carnival every year."

I was gonna' say something else, but before I could get the words out of my mouth, I heard a sound that I had hoped I would never hear again.

"Nope," I thought to myself. "It cannot be. I refuse to believe it."

But I looked at Dakota and Meranda and could tell from their faces that they had heard it too.

I slowly turned my head and coming right at us, zooming like buzzards after road kill, were Stix and Chief Braxton. Chief Braxton still had the scarf wrapped around his neck and he was barking like a maniac. Stix was laughing, and had that look in his eye that made goose-bumps pop out all over my body. Oh. No. Here we go again…

I glanced over at Meranda. Looked her straight in her eyes, and knew that she was remembering, like I was, the talk we had had the night before. While 'Kota was off doing something else, we had sat on the beach and talked about what we would do if Stix and his dog, or any other danger, approached us again. And M had shared some things about her self that I hadn't known before. We both knew what we had to do.

I put my hand on 'Kota's waist and pulled him behind me. Meranda flew up to us and we floated upright – shoulder to shoulder – facing the crazed-looking boy and his maniacal dog. I heard Meranda's beautiful voice – I could see why she was in the celestial choir – loudly chanting in a language I did not understand, and had not heard her use before. It sounded good, though, and powerful.

And I started with my part. No sounds no words, just pushing, with everything in me, energy. Right at the two in front of us. With a smile on my face I focused on my heart and shot love right out of it onto Stix and Chief Braxton. They both skidded to a stop, inches away from us. I could tell that Chief Braxton was still trying to move forward but he couldn't. He kept making the motions of moving forward, but they weren't working. He couldn't even bark. And poor Stix – yep, I almost felt sorry for him – wasn't trying to do anything. He couldn't move, and the shock on his face was worth a gazillion dollars. They were frozen just like statues.

I could feel Dakota behind me, drawing in big gulp after big gulp of air and I knew that his face probably looked a lot like Stix's. M and I looked at each other, nodded slightly, then turned around and resumed our journey. I turned around after a few minutes and saw that the two knuckle-heads were in the same place that we'd left them. Statue-like. After a few more minutes of floating along like everything was normal, I stopped. I couldn't take it anymore and my gut was about to bust. And I knew that Dakota was gonna' split wide open if we didn't stop.

Meranda and I high-fived and started laughing our fool heads off! We spun and twirled and danced and I grabbed an imaginary microphone and starting wailing Bob Marley's song: "Don't worry, about a thing… cuz'a every little thing, is gonna' be alright." Poor Dakota was just floating there in one spot - looking about as confused as it was possible to look. He kept turning and looking behind him, expecting, I knew, for Stix and Chief Braxton to appear at any moment. It was hard for Meranda and I to stop celebrating, but we knew we had to – to help get 'Kota out of his shock.

"What, Erik??" he screamed at me, pulling on the arm of my tee-shirt. "What in the world happened back there!? How did you guys make them stop? I know it was you because as soon as you started singing, Meranda, and you started smiling and staring at them with that look on your face, Erik, they stopped in mid-air! What were you doing? Oh my God!"

"Come on, little brother. Let's go sit on that cloud over there and talk." M and I each put our arms through one of Dakota's and floated with him between us, to a nice fat fluffy cloud and sat him on it. We plopped down on either side of him. As happy as I know that he was on the inside, for having escaped those horrible ones, the shock of what he'd seen was wearing on him. We had to explain pretty fast.

"Last night," I started, "while you were hanging out with the lobster fishermen, M and I started talking about Love. She told me some of the things she was taught by her mother and grandmother. One of them being about the power of Love. They were healers, you know, and they knew that Love had a most powerful effect on the healing process. It was one of the things they used on their patients, along with the herbs and massage and stuff. They always focused Love on them, and when they did, the healing happened so much faster. So they came to realize how powerful that energy is, and started using it for a lot of things. When there were arguments or disagreements between people in the village, they brought in the Love, and things got squared away real quick, with everybody feeling good about it. They taught everybody in the village about it and the next time people came and tried to take over and do bad things in their village, all the people shot Love at them and they couldn't advance any further against them!"

"That's right," Meranda chimed in. "We became the most peaceful and happy village in the area, and everybody started coming to us to find out what we were doing. And of course we were happy to teach everybody, and soon that whole part of the country started changing. The crops got better. Rain came when we needed it, and the villages were more friendly with each other, exchanging things that everybody needed, and stuff like that."

"Yep. And then when she was telling me all of that, I remembered some of the stuff that Mama used to say to us, like how important it was for us to care for each other, and other people. I remember her saying once that Love makes the world go 'round. I didn't know what she meant, but I started getting it when me and M were talking. It was Love that kept us all together when that crazy man was living with us. So we thought we'd give it a try; next time we needed it. And it worked!"

142

"Wow!" 'Kota shouted. "Well why didn't you tell us this a long time ago, Meranda, and what was that you were singing?!"

"Well, I really didn't think much about it until Erik and I were talking about that skunk Stix and how we could protect ourselves if he showed up again. Then I remembered. So next time, Dakota, you're gonna' have to stand with us, and focus on your heart, and just push Love out of it, with all your might."

"That'll be easy for my brother," I laughed. "He's about the loving-est person I know!" I reached out and ruffled 'Kota's hair, and he looked at me with those big brown eyes of his. I knew this talk had changed everything for him. He was gonna be all about the Love after this.

"But what were you saying, Meranda?" he had to know.

"I was speaking in my tribal language. I only use that when I really need to, cuz it reminds me of home, and makes me a little sad. But it gives me so much power, cuz I'm drawing on all of my family and my ancestors, my land, and the All There Is, or God, as some people call it. I was repeating, over and over, "Love is All There is, Love is All There is." Cuz it really is. It's everything."

CPSIA information can be obtained
at www.ICGtesting.com
Printed in the USA
BVHW092321021121
620554BV00020B/1017